The Gun War

Gun Grabbers Incite a Revolutionary War Where Establishment Politicians Die One by One.

A Political Thriller Novel

Alan Fensin

http://thegunwar.com

This book is a work of fiction. Names, characters, places and incidents are products of the authors' imaginations and are used fictitiously. Any resemblance to actual events, locales, or persons, living or dead, is entirely coincidental.

ISBN 1-57706-663-4
ISBN 978-1-57706-663-7

Published by:
Burlington Book Division, Burlington National
United States of America

Table of Contents

Prologue

In the not too distant future, President Cramer and various advisors intently listened to the senate row call for the recently signed United Nations Safety Treaty. The senate would need a total of sixty-seven yes votes for the treaty to pass. The vote was so close it appeared it would go down to the wire.

Some senators objected to the clause in the treaty that said, "The type of firearms a civilian can buy and own is determined by the United Nations Technical Committee." But they were assured that this was only about fully automatic guns and newly developed types of magnetic and laser weapons. Still, many of the senators were not convinced.

When the last senator voted yes President Cramer let out an audible sigh of relief. The long denied political establishment's objective of gun control would soon be American law. With all the guns confiscated, the administration could consolidate its power and have complete control. No one would be able to interfere with President Cramer's decisions. With the Bill of Rights out of the way he could fulfill his destiny to better control America.

A month later the Supreme Court announced their ruling on the treaty controversy. Gun rights justices argued that amendments take precedence over anything in the constitution so logically a treaty can't affect gun rights. However, along party lines the court voted six to three that because of Article VI in the Constitution the signed treaty would take precedence over the second amendment and be the supreme law of the land.

President Cramer then decreed, "All guns will be confiscated by means of a mandatory buyback. Everyone has three months to turn in their guns and ammunition. For each gun you will be paid between one hundred and five hundred dollars. After three months, gun owners will be criminals. Law enforcement teams will make arrests and forcibly confiscate the guns and jail the offenders."

Retaining freedom has been a constant struggle. And Americans will not easily give up their Bill of Rights because of some treaty. America is a country founded on freedom and constitutional law. If the new treaty was used to confiscate guns, this power grab would not end peacefully.

A new unknown militia was formed to fight the global government power grab. America now stood on the brink of war as the political establishment begins seizing firearms by force.

When America was born thirteen colonies believed they could defeat the British Army, then the most powerful army and navy on Earth. Miraculously, they did.

Could a new untested small militia repeat this and beat the vastly more powerful American law enforcement and military establishment? Freedom and lives depended on the outcome.

Chapter 1

"It was a horrible day, a really horrible day," Dr. Birch reflected. "I was making my rounds at the hospital when a nurse told me to look at the news. At first, I thought it was just a crime report of someone killed in yet another police raid as the government goons tried to confiscate everyone's guns. I didn't see how it could affect me. Then I saw the name. It was my son's name."

"Even then, I thought it was someone else with the same name. I immediately called my son's cell but there was no answer. Then I phoned his wife's cell and found out that he had indeed been killed. She said that without warning, government agents broke into their house at four in the morning. That's the favorite time for fascists to stage no-knock home invasions. They stormed in and tossed flash grenades around and shot my son when he was still lying in bed. I was at a loss for words. All I could say to her was, 'No, no, no.'

"For a long while, I hoped that this was wrong and that he was still alive. It wasn't until I actually saw his body that I accepted his murder. He was innocent of any crime, and still they shot him like a sleeping dog. The pain came in waves, sometimes weaker, sometimes stronger. It bent me over, and then knocked me down. It felt like my life was opened up and I was forced to look at all the gears, switches and blood inside that's called life. My fists were sore from pounding on my desk. Oh God, I thought, how could some stupid crime like this be happening in America?" Dr. Birch stopped talking and watched the eyes of his patient, Craig Miles.

Craig looked at Dr. Birch and thought this was a strange way for a doctor to talk. Dr. Ralph Birch was Craig's oncologist, treating him for cancer. All their other talks concerned cancer, medication and lifestyle changes.

Craig's cancer was inoperable but if he used the right medication and treatments, he could live perhaps a couple more years. Still the end might be extremely painful and difficult. The feeling of immortality that he once had was gone. Now, he could picture his own death, and it scared him.

"Doctor I'm sorry for your loss. Bad things sometimes happen."

Dr. Birch nodded in acknowledgement but wasn't finished with his monologue. "Not a single day goes by that I don't remember the police killing of my son. The American government has turned into a terrorist organization.

"I loved my son completely. He was a good boy. He was so good. He was my life and to have him murdered that way. The impossible happened. My world was turned upside down. My head felt ready to explode. I had the worst headaches that came from the stress and anger that the Federal Government created in me. It was too much.

"My life will never be the same. I miss him so very much. I used to love, and smile and save lives. But now my miserable bleak life is without meaning and seems hopeless. I had to take a two-week leave of absence from the hospital. I couldn't believe this could happen to me. I will never forget. I will never forgive. Why? Why? Oh God, why?"

"Doctor, again I'm truly sorry for your loss, but we should be talking about my cancer treatment."

A confused look came over his face and he rocked back and forth in his chair. "I am no longer a father and now I will never be a grandfather. I grieve every day of my life."

Dr. Birch paused for a few seconds, but before Craig could say anything else, Dr. Birch continued, "It didn't make sense. All I got was a hollow and unsatisfying answer from my minister. He said that God never gives us more pain than we can take. He said that God knew I could handle it. Does that mean that Brian's death is my fault for being a strong person? I blamed myself because I was so strong that God thought I could handle it."

"After that, I left the church. They failed me in my time of need. What occurred on April 21st has changed my life forever." There was a look of sorrow and despair on Dr. Birch's face. His eyes were wet and he was fighting back tears and he finally stopped talking.

Craig worked as a pharmacist area supervisor for a large drug store chain in the greater Washington, DC area. He managed to spend everything he made and had no real savings. Before he got sick, his hobbies were Jack Daniels, and gambling, mostly slot machines and sometimes roulette. His fondness for gambling casinos cost him a bundle, and he worried about making ends meet. More than worried, Craig was scared to death. Craig had a family and what would happen to them? What would his family do without his income? How would they pay the house note? How will they survive?

Craig knew life was short, but, like most people, he lived his life as if it would never end. Like most people, he deceived himself about the truth of life and death. He occupied his mind with the umpteen million things that actually meant virtually nothing when compared with his inevitable and quickly approaching death.

Craig wondered if he would ever understand the meaning of life and death. Was his whole life to end this way with no explanation? Was life a movie where God would not show you the last ten minutes of the film? Before, Craig never thought about these things, but since his cancer diagnosis that's all that occupy his thoughts.

"Craig I have set an appointment for you with a psychiatrist."

"Doc, I don't need to see a shrink."

"I require every one of my potential terminal patients to do this. It might help and might not, but please do it for me."

"Okay Doc as long as everyone does it I'll go."

"Craig one more thing. We have to talk. Could you meet me for lunch later this week?"

Craig was stunned. His time was running out and Dr. Birch wanted to meet for lunch. They hadn't even discussed his condition. What could his doctor possibly want to discuss over lunch?

"Well, Doc, I gotta tell you. I'm a little confused. I feel bad about your son and all, but shouldn't we be discussing my situation?"

Dr. Birch paused for a few seconds and with an expression of anxiety, looked at a picture of his son on the wall. "At lunch, I'd like to talk a little bit more about my son, but that conversation mainly concerns your condition, your finances and a way we can help each other. Something has to happen to save America, and we can be part of it."

Craig tried again to offer his sympathy concerning the terrible disaster that happened to Dr. Birch's son, but Dr. Birch continued to press, "Can you meet me?"

"Okay," said Craig, with an exasperated sigh and a thoughtful nod. "What time and where?"

"Wednesday at the JJ's Lobster and Steak Room around noon. I will be in their small private dinning room. And read this short Militia of One brochure tonight, so we can discuss it. This brochure may solve some of your financial problems.

After Craig left, Dr. Birch continued to sit for some time, idly rapping a pencil on the top of his desk. Dr. Birch felt a tremendous satisfaction from the events he had set in motion. He also felt tired and, in some way, really lonely. He would have liked to talk to his murdered son and tell him that his revenge against President Cramer and the terrorist police force had begun.

Chapter 2

State Times Post News, Digital Edition: Keep America safe and turn in you guns.

Have you handed in your illegal firearms? If not, this is the final extension. You only have until May 31st to turn them in. After that you will be classified as a felon and your home will be subject to no-knock, middle of the night inspections. This could result in your death or that of loved ones. You will also be prosecuted under the new laws and convicted as a felon. Do not be a felon. Do not go to jail. Turn in your guns now.

Thinking about the upcoming with Dr. Birch exhausted Craig. It was rush hour and on the way home he almost had a serious wreck. He absent-mindedly merged on to Dulles Access Road and didn't see that he cut off a driver and missed hitting him by inches. The other driver shook his fist at him and then shot him the finger. Craig thought that people were really getting crazy and slowed down. He would be happy when this damn miserable day ended.

The summer night was hot and aggravated Craig's negative disposition. He had a bad feeling about the meeting with Dr. Birch. And he was beginning to wonder about Dr. Birch himself. The only logical idea he got was that Dr. Birch must want something from him, but Craig had no idea what that could possibly be.

Outwardly, Craig appeared to be a successful pharmacist area manager. He supervised five of his company's pharmacies in the greater Washington, DC area. He had a six figure salary and lived in a charming brick Colonial style house located in Reston, Virginia, approximately forty minutes from Washington.

Craig walked purposefully up the flagstone lighted walkway and stepped into the spotlessly clean home. As usual, Snowball, a thirteen-pound Bichon Frise, was the first to hear him. She growled and barked a few seconds, then realized who it was. She immediately wagged her tail as she made a beeline for Craig. He stooped down, and Snowball bounded into his arms. Craig hugged her, knowing that Snowball could always be counted on for unconditional love.

The old leather chair squeaked as Craig collapsed into it. Snowball immediately jumped into his lap. As Craig hugged Snowball, he asked himself how many birthdays and Christmas seasons he had missed while working late at the drug store? He always said he worked such long hours for the family, but he knew he could have been home more. Some of that time away was hanging out at the bar, gambling or chasing women.

His wife Joan was in her late forties, ten years younger than Craig. She had an uncommon strength that allowed her to overlook Craig's little boy ways. She was a gentle woman, full of compassion for

Craig. Even that one time when she discovered his dalliances with another woman, she was kind. He said he was sorry and would never do it again and she forgave him. Since his illness, Craig wondered why those sexual encounters ever had power over him. Maybe it was the medication or the worry about his impending death, but now erotic images and thoughts quickly dissipated and held no appeal.

Joan had a youthful quality of innocence in her knowing eyes that made her seem younger than she was. "How are you feeling?" Joan asked with a warm heart felt smile as she entered the living room. She knew that Craig had recently complained of the steady decline of his stamina and strength.

It was a strange time, it was a totally bizarre time, but Craig knew that his destiny was inescapable. He knew he couldn't tell Joan the truth of his impending death. "I still don't feel great, but I'm doing better today," he said quietly.

Kerwood, their two year old daughter, ran into the living room and raised her hands, indicating the desire to be held. Craig picked her up and delighted in her youthful exuberance. It was easier to pick Kerwood up than put her down, but after the third try she let go and Craig set her down.

Craig gave Joan a hug and a light peck on the mouth. He looked at Joan and said, "Your eyes, they look so red. Have you been crying?"

"No," she lied. "My allergies kick in this time of the year and cause my eyes to look red." Craig accepted this answer because he didn't want to think of the alternative.

Craig had no intention of telling Joan the truth concerning his cancer. If he did she would look at their finances, and they were a disaster. He wanted to put that off as long as possible. He knew that Joan would try to tell him what to do, so better not to even bring it up. He would shield her from the true hopelessness of their situation.

Joan noticed that Craig had recently developed sadness in his eyes and a defeatist slump in his shoulders. "You have to keep a positive mind," she said as her eyes glistened.

"What do I have to be positive about?"

"Craig!" replied Joan in a strong voice. It was a request for him to understand that he could have a positive attitude regardless of the circumstances he was in.

"Be an optimist. Last week I read a story titled the definition of an optimist. It took place long ago in Bourbon, France."

"A thief was caught in the act of a capital crime and hauled up before the king, who asked, 'Is there any reason why I shouldn't hang you tomorrow morning?'"

"The thief knew that the king had a favorite horse. So the thief fell to his knees before the king and pleaded, 'Oh your majesty, you are making a huge mistake. I am so skilled with horses that if you spare me, in one year I could teach your favorite horse to speak.'"

"The king thought this over and said, 'I will give you the year to perform such a miracle, but if you fail, your death will be swift.'"

The Gun War

"So the thief went to the stables to start teaching the horse to talk. A friend asked, 'Why did you promise the king such a stupid thing? You know you can't teach that horse to talk.'"

"The thief smiled and replied, 'Instead of dying tomorrow I will be alive for at least one year more. One year is a long time. In that year the king might be overthrown or die, the horse might die, I might die of natural causes, or who knows, the horse might talk. And I know that in life, every moment must be treasured.'"

"Craig, " Joan said, "you have to look at the possibilities and never give up. Remember, the horse might talk."

Craig nodded in agreement and smiled, but he knew that his situation was not the same. The man in the story wasn't going to have months of excruciating pain. But Craig knew that he would. He knew he was going to die, but he still had difficulties accepting that he deserved it.

Today they were closer than they had been for some years. The wood fireplace crackled, and its romantic flickering light played on the ceiling. But there were secrets they kept from each other, and therefore, they did not have true communication. He never told her that because of his sins the family had no real savings and after he died she would have to sell the house.

He looked back over the years of his marriage and knew he had not been a good husband. Maybe his terminal illness was God's punishment for his gambling, drinking and adultery over the years.

Maybe some final sacrifice could turn the tally back in his favor.

Craig said, "I have to get up early tomorrow so I'm going to bed now."

When he stood up, he immediately turned his back to Joan so she could not see the look of sadness on his face. There were tears in his eyes, and they started to run down his cheeks. He quickly walked down the hall to the bathroom, got a Kleenex, and blew his nose.

Before going to sleep, he got out the short "Militia of One" brochure that Dr. Birch had given him and headed upstairs. He put on his reading glasses and began to read.

Militia Of One

By John Grayson

"This country, with its institutions, belongs to the people who inhabit it. Whenever they shall grow weary of the existing Government, they can exercise their constitutional right of amending it, or their revolutionary right to dismember or overthrow it." - Abraham Lincoln, First inaugural address, March 4 1861

Militia of One Manifesto

Freedom and liberty are the predominant themes of American history. It is only through individual freedom that we are allowed to explore our reason for being and grow into our full potential. It is what generations of Americans have lived and died for. The power to keep that freedom and liberty comes from the barrel of a gun.

The ruling establishment in Washington lacks constitutional legitimacy to take our guns. But still they order us to turn them in. We refuse and will fight and we will take back our freedom. This manifesto is about how to protect our constitution and to eliminate the people who pervert it. We will eliminate those leaders who want to grab our guns.

We have a terrorist President, a lawless Congress and a lawless Supreme Court. They use the cover of the United Nations Treaty to ignore the second, the fourth, and the fifth amendments of our constitution. In their search for guns, they break into people's homes while they are asleep, killing and otherwise terrorizing them.

All American law comes from our Constitution, and all laws that ignore it are fiction. Giving up our bill or rights is one of those fictions that will not be allowed to stand. Any change to our Bill of Rights requires a constitutional amendment.

President Cramer wants to take us down the path towards global socialism and away from our constitutional republic. Those establishment politicians who sold out their sworn allegiance to the American Constitution for money and power are traitors.

The United National Treaty does not change the second amendment, which was approved four years after our Constitution was signed. It takes precedence over anything in the Constitution and any treaty. Therefore only a new amendment can take away our freedom to keep and bear arms. Allowing the global government to outlaw the critical protections of our Bill of Rights is illegal and totally unacceptable.

The Gun War

President Cramer swore to obey and protect the Constitution. But instead Cramer ignored it. Gun grabbing police now break into our homes with often-deadly consequences. We refuse to take it anymore. We want our country back from the United Nation dictators.

For our loved ones and for all freedom loving Americans this gun rights infringement must end. We will fight for our constitutional rights, our freedom and our guns! This is our declaration of war!

Beginning this July 4th there will be only one question. How many gun-grabbing terrorists will we have to eliminate before they obey our Constitution and leave our Bill of Rights, our guns and our freedom alone?

Rules for the Militia of One Operatives

If the politicians don't obey the Constitution, then we won't obey their laws that come from the Constitution. So until we win, there are no government laws.

The gun grabbers are terrorists and break into our homes, killing our families. We are not terrorists, so the first rule is to keep collateral damage to a minimum. However collateral damage will inevitably occur, especially for bodyguards and immediate friends and family of the targets to be eliminated.

Targets

The following list of people will all be targeted:

- Politicians, judges and high-ranking government individuals who voted or ruled to steal our guns
- Key people who support the gun grab with their money
- UN officials still in America

We are now at the point where only blood will wash away the guilt of the government terrorists. Members of the Militia will use covert elimination of individual targets. They will encompass many new types of attacks never before used. Since we have no leaders, we are impossible to stop. As the carnage of gun grabbers multiplies there will come a time when they will accept our terms for peace.

If there is one thing that America stands for it is freedom. Untold numbers of Americans have died to protect it. The elite establishment government has slowly eroded our freedom and gotten away with it. But now, in one quick run, they have brazenly chosen to eradicate our Bill of Rights. This time they crossed a bridge too far.

We fought the revolutionary war against an unelected king and replaced him with the a Constitutional Republic. Why would we surrender our Constitution to unelected United Nation bureaucrats? Ignoring our Constitutions bill of rights is surrendering to tyranny. We will never surrender. It's time to explain the facts of life and death to the Washington political establishment.

The Gun War

The millions of members of the Militia of One hereby declare war on that establishment.

Attacks Concepts

- Do not talk about the Militia of One except to immediate teammates.
- The size of your group should be no more than three.
- Break off the attack if it becomes too risky, and have a plan for a safe retreat.
- Destroy all incriminating evidence as soon as possible.

Terms for Peace

The Cramer administration became the aggressor when they began to attack and kill honest citizens. The gun war will end when they cease hostilities and agree that our constitution is above any United Nations laws. You will know it is a real peace if they accept all our terms:

- They renounce the United Nations Treaty treaty taking our guns and accept that the Second Amendment is the law of the land.
- They agree to pardon every Militia of One member and immediately release all our prisoners of war.
- They agree that if these terms are not respected, we will go back to the attack with increased ferocity.

All those who choose to join me and start their own group are welcome to the Militia of One.

John Grayson

This was the brochure that Craig had been hearing about for weeks. It was transmitted from person to person, until many millions had read it. It was also all over the Internet. But Craig had never read it until now.

It was a short read, and when Craig put the brochure down he was mystified. Why in the world did Dr. Birch want him to read this thing? Did Dr. Birch know that he wasn't particularly political and he doesn't even own a gun? Perhaps Dr. Birch mistook him for someone else. When they had lunch in a couple of days he would ask the good doctor why this Militia of One nonsense concerned him.

Chapter 3

State Times Post News, Digital Edition: Senator Sharpless and two others were killed at a stoplight. A motorcycle drove up next to their limousine. When the light changed the unknown rider in a black leather suit tossed a modified M18A1 Claymore directional mine onto the car's roof. As the motorcycle roared away a huge explosion erupted behind it, and the Limo blew into pieces. The "towards the enemy" side had magnets attached so it landed correctly on the roof and exploded seconds later. The ball bearings backed by C-4 plastic explosive ripped through the roof and killed everyone inside. One witness said the motorcycle didn't have a license plate. The witness also reported the driver wore a helmet with its dark visor obscuring his face.

In an interview President Sam Cramer said, "The Militia of One is ridiculous. There is no way these few crazies can stand up to Homeland Security, the FBI and similar organizations, let alone the might of our armed forces. These jokers can run but they can't hide from the unlimited power and resources of the United States."

Karen Mehurin owned Firearm Training and Sales, a very successful gun store and state of the art indoor shooting range in Fredericksburg. Her husband had started it, but he died when his National Guard unit was called up to fight in the

Muslim religious wars in Iraq. In his absence, Karen took over. It was a difficult time but she made the store bigger, better and a lot more profitable.

Karen was only average looking but knew that in today's world, society favors the beautiful and better-looking people. So Karen had her nose made smaller, her breasts bigger and her lips fuller.

In the past, people who visited Firearm Training and Sales had come away very impressed with its professionalism and clean modern facilities. It was a big top-notch gun store. A large number of expensive waist-high display glass cases had once been filled with numerous brands and styles of handguns. But now they were empty.

The twenty lane shooting range was in the basement where stray shots would be contained by the dirt outside of the range. Clean climate controlled air was pumped into each lane, and all nitrate gases from firearms were swiftly removed. But it too was empty.

The huge display area normally held all manner of guns related equipment. The adjacent training center has the latest audio/video projection equipment with a hundred very comfortable chairs.

But life got difficult for Karen. The Federal government was in the process of visiting every gun dealer and expropriating their gun inventory and shutting them down. There were 130,000 licensed gun dealers in America. Almost 60,000 were retail stores. So Karen had a few more days before they get to her. But the clock was ticking fast. Fortunately, her guns and ammunition quickly sold out as soon as the treaty was signed. She didn't have to replace them because that would soon be illegal. Consequently, she had a serious amount of money in the bank. But she still owes a large mortgage on the building, and in the current climate, it was impossible to sell a shooting range for anything approaching its real value.

Two months earlier, when Karen realized the political establishment would shut down her store, it had made her sorrowful. But she did not sit and cry. She had enough of that when her husband died, when there was nothing she could do. Now she was just plain angry. And with that anger, she decided she had to do something to help defeat the anti-gun political establishment enemies.

Butch Hunter smiled as he entered the store and greeted Karen. Her sensually augmented body really worked on him. He thought she was seriously beautiful. He looked at her empty display cases and said, "I can't tell you how unhappy I am that they are closing you down. It's definitely not right. You had a legal business, and they shut you down."

Karen's lips parted in a joyful smile. "Unfortunately this will be your last shooting self-defense class. But I'm sure something will change, and this new law will not last. The American people won't give up their freedom because some dubious law said they had to."

"I hope you're right, but so many people are afraid to stand up to the government. The way I see it—"

Karen interrupted with a glance at her watch, "Hunter, your assistant Patrick and the students have all arrived. Lets discuss this later."

"But I want to find out what you think about the Militia of One."

Karen shook her head no and put a finger to her lips to indicate silence and then to her ear as if someone was listening.

"However since this is the last class, I should be on time," said Hunter and he entered the large meeting room.

The students immediately settled down when they saw Hunter. He was a retired Marine major. At about six foot six, he had broad shoulders, a thick neck and ramrod straight posture. Something about his demeanor was one of being in charge and demanding respect. It might be his military bearing, or it might be his size but he is obviously not a person you would want to have an argument with.

Hunter looked around the room and nodded. "Since the new United Nations laws will be shutting down this gun store and shooting range, this will be our last class. And because of the new law, we will skip the combat shooting today. I am pleased that my assistant Patrick did such a great job teaching you the fine art of accurate shooting in stressful situations. He is really a great shot, isn't he? He was also a great Marine gunny who consistently thought outside the box.

"Remember his instructions. Find cover or move while you shoot. Concealment is not as good as cover because bullets can go through concealment but not through cover."

One student raised his hand and asked, "Can you give an example of cover?"

"Sure. Examples of good cover are behind the engine block of a car, behind a large tree, behind a brick wall or anything else that will stop a bullet from passing through.

"This final lesson is the most important one. You of course know that the deadline to turn in all guns was two weeks ago. We will assume that this United Nations gun control madness will not last very long, and then you will again be able to carry a gun. I say this because there is now a movement to change that law. I am referring to the Militia of One flier that probably you have all read. I'm also going to say some things you will never hear anywhere else. So listen up.

"This is for those who didn't turn all or even some of your guns in to the gun police. You should know that gun dealers are required to keep twenty years of records of who bought which gun. Many dealers will never dispose of even older records. The government is now collecting these records. The government will computerize them, and soon know exactly what guns you bought."

Another student asked, "Does that mean that our guns will be automatically registered?"

"It sure does. Your guns that you bought from a gun store in the last thirty years are now registered. So if the gun grabbers come to your house, they will come in heavy with superior numbers and the element of surprise. Do not resist, because you will not win. If you do keep guns and ammo make sure they will not be found. Bury or hide the gun and ammo close to metal so metal detectors will not be able to find them."

Another student asked, "But they know we have the gun so what is the use of hiding it?"

"That's why a good idea is to pre-write a fake bill of sale and have someone sign it using a bogus name. This way you can immediately show the authorities that the gun in question is no longer yours. Even if they can't locate the new owner, you are off the hook.

"One of the most important things you have to learn is what to do in case you have to shoot someone in self-defense. The first thing is to leave the scene and destroy and get rid of the gun. Remember it is now illegal to possess guns. Disassemble the gun and beat the gun barrel with a hammer.

"The second thing is not to say anything except that you want your lawyer. Remember, anything you say will be used against you, so don't say anything except to ask for your lawyer.

'The third thing to be aware of is just because you fired your weapon in self-defense, you are not legally allowed to even have a gun. If you stick around, you will probably go to jail and the criminal's relatives will sue you in civil court for every penny you have or will ever make. In civil court you don't have all the legal protections of our Bill of Rights. You could easily spend a small fortune defending yourself. And if you win, the attorney costs could force you into bankruptcy. And if you lose you will lose everything."

"That's not fair!" yelled one of the students, and the other students agreed.

"Yes, but that's the way the system works. To protect yourself, leave the area immediately. If they do manage to find you, tell them you were afraid for your life and he had friends with guns so you left as fast as you could. But never admit to firing a gun or even having one. The bottom line here is that now guns are illegal and you need to protect yourself.

"Are there any questions that you have been waiting you whole life to ask? This may be your last chance."

The only female student, who once worked in law enforcement, stood. "I want to know more about the FBI's computer they call AFIS. One of our detectives told me that it could identify a gun and the owner from either the bullet or the spent brass without even having the gun. Is that true?"

"Pretty much. The way it works gun manufacturers are required to take photographs of every bullet's rifling and also of the ejection markings and microscopic firing pin markings on the spent brass. Since the year 2000, this information has been loaded into the AFIS fingerprint computer.

"After the gun is fired a few hundred times or so the markings do change slightly. So the computer will likely show more than one match. This is especially true of a popular model that sells hundreds of thousands guns. So just because your gun was a match does not mean you will be convicted in a court of law.

"So this system is not perfect, and there may be more than one match. But this still gives law enforcement a very good idea of a few people in a particular location who possibly own the gun in question. Once they have a few names, there are many more bits of information readily available.

"A good detective will get your picture, address etc. from your driver's license and other data files. Face detection software matches your picture against the many cameras in the area. They show your picture to every witness and even though you may be totally and completely innocent, often a witness wanting to help the police will say that it was you.

"The detective will also get your car's license plate number and match it against the numbers from the stop light cameras and other cameras in and around the crime area. Your cell phone number will be used to determine which cell tower you were near at the time of the shooting. They can triangulate your location very closely.

"Officers find the actual gun about half the time when they search your home. Of course this means go directly to jail and do not pass go. But they also check any ammunition batch numbers, your cloths for nitrate exposure, etc. and build a case against you for having an illegal gun.

"Don't forget the forensic trace evidence. These are items such as DNA, hair, fibers, dirt, pollen, and other types of information. They can all be worthless unless there is a suspect to match against. If you are a suspect, they try to match them against you. Sometimes, even though you may be innocent, they come up with a false positive match. Then you have a problem. So you really don't want to be a suspect. And remember to keep your mouth shut. Don't tell anyone you have a gun. Most cases aren't solved by good detective work, but instead by someone tipping off the police. Any other questions?"

"Do you approve of laser sights?"

"Definitively. This is especially true for a small pistol that has only a few inches sight radius between the front and the rear sight. The laser sight radius is greatly extended from those few inches to many yards. It makes aiming the pistol in high stress situations more accurate. And when you don't have cover and you're in a running gunfight, it is much easier to shoot and stay on target. Naturally, you have to practice both with and without lasers since the battery might be dead at a time when you need it most. Anything else?"

One student asked, "Why is President Cramer trying to take our guns away?"

"It really doesn't matter why they want our guns. Guns are an emotional issue to some people. But that's not a good, logical reason. The only thing that actually and legally matters is that our Bill of Rights says, 'The right of the people to keep and bear arms shall not be infringed.' America would have to ratify a new constitutional amendment to legally take our guns. Either pass a new amendment, like they did with alcohol prohibition when the Eighteenth Amendment establishing prohibition was reversed by the Twenty-first amendment, or leave our guns alone. Our constitutional rights can not be denied because of the emotions of the moment. And that is the bottom line."

Two hours later the class ended. Patrick and the students said their final good goodbyes and left. However, Hunter wanted to finish his conversation with Karen, and was in no hurry to leave. He asked her, "Are you going to sell the building or rent it out to someone else?"

Karen gave Hunter an annoyed look, and for the second time that day she put a finger to her lips to indicate silence.

The Gun War

Chapter 4

State Times Post News, Digital Edition: A hybrid weapon called a "Bow Mag" seriously wounded Senator Johnson. Once widely available at many retailers they are now illegal. However, there are still over a million in circulation and there is no records of who owns them.

Senator Johnson's injuries are not life threatening, but she will probably not be able to return to the senate.

The Bow Mag is an exploding arrowhead mounted on the tip of the arrow and fired by a standard bow. When the arrow hits a target, the stopping momentum pushes a firing pin into the 357 Magnum cartridge at the tip of the arrow, causing it to explode. The Bow Mag discharges upon impact and adds its energy and hot gasses to the arrow's momentum when striking the target.

A piece of paper wrapped around the shaft of the arrow had a printed message that said, "You don't need a gun to shoot someone." There are currently no suspects in this crime.

Still annoyed, Karen said, "Let's go into the office and discuss it." Karen pulled the door behind them.

"Now I am still working on getting my anger under control. It was not enough that my husband was killed in Iraq. Now they are taking his business and my livelihood away. I catch myself slamming doors shut, kicking garbage cans and snapping at people.

"I'm still considering my options, so for now I'll keep the merchandise I have left. I don't believe our country will allow our Bill of Rights to be trampled on like the United Nations is doing. I hope this madness will change, and then I'll open up my store again.

"The reason I wanted to talk in here is because we found a bug in the show room. We left it there and swept the office, and the rest of the area was clean. But we can't talk out there."

Hunter didn't believe the government would stoop so low as to use an illegal bug at a gun shop, but he asked, "Do you think there will be a revolution?"

"Oh definitely, it has already started. You're the one who asked about the Militia of One. As you also probably know they are very small groups with no central control or chain of command.

"For now the news media is mostly ignoring it or playing it down. They want us to have the mindset that any resistance is pointless and will fail. However, the bodies are beginning to pile up fast, and they can't keep ignoring it much longer. I think the gun confiscation will have to end.

"The concept of independent small fighting groups is different that any other civil war. I think that sort of individualistic guerrilla war could easily beat the government. You saw a lot of combat with the Marines in Iraq. What do you think?"

"You could be right," said Hunter. When I attended the Marine Corps War College they had a required list of books to read. You would expect books like *The Art of War, The Prince, On War* and *The History of the Peloponnesian War*. They were there. But others would surprise you. One that comes to mind is *Starship Troopers*, a 1959 science fiction novel by Robert Heinlein.

"From what I recall, Starship Troopers was a science fiction novel about a war with alien bugs from another planet. Killing the bug solders or workers would never end the war. The bug queens and leaders lived one thousand feet under the earth and were almost impossible to get to.

"The bug queens produced large quantities of worker and soldier bugs that went to the surface to work and fight. Killing them made no different since the queens didn't care and quickly produced more. Only killing the well protected underground bug queens and leaders would work to win the war. Of course that was not easy to do.

"Also, the overall theme of the book seemed to be that social responsibility requires individual sacrifice. So a group of smart and dedicated individuals, fighting for the same goal, can beat a much larger better-equipped centrally controlled army by attacking the command structure. That is the basic definition of guerilla warfare. And the Militia of One war is actually a guerilla war.

"One quote from the book that I recall said something like 'war is constructive violence for our purpose'. The Militia of One uses violence against only the opposition leaders who want to take our freedom away. In this war the leaders can't send their disposable soldiers to die. They must die themselves. So yes, there is no doubt in my mind that if the Militia of One is able to stay the course they will win. However, progress may be slow as most people usually wait to see which way the wind is blowing before committing to anything this serious.

"However over one hundred million Americans own guns. So I expect a large number of them will fight to protect our bill of rights and constitutional freedoms. Even if only one percent of one hundred million would join the militia, it would be a huge million person fighting machine. And the concept of this type of individual revolution by huge numbers of dedicated groups is unheard of in all of history. And these Militia men are already very embedded into society and fighting for their freedom.

"I know of no current army that could stand up to them. Armies weren't trained to fight a Militia of One type of war."

"Good response," Karen said. "That's what I thought too. But it's good to hear you confirm it. I'm curious why you left the Marines."

"I don't know why everyone wants to know that. But the short answer is that I was a major for many years. If I wasn't promoted to a Lt. Colonel or even a full Colonel at the end of twenty years, then I was probably stuck as a Major forever. It made more sense to get out and start receiving retirement money.

"I would have a whole lot more freedom, and if I get bored I can always get a job in private industry. They like midlevel military officers there.

"I had over twenty years of active duty, so I could retire with more than half pay. This is more than forty thousand a year. And more importantly, it began immediately after my separation. I didn't have to wait until I was sixty-five. Also, there is a small cost of living increase each year.

"Finally, and this was the key, I was getting disillusioned with why we were in Iraq. Our initial victory in the second Iraq war was swift because much of their military just stood down. One of Iraq's top generals told me that as soon as we captured Saddam Hussein and all their weapons of mass destruction he was told that America would give the country back to them and they could choose a leader from among their ranks.

"It made sense that we would want a strong Iraq because the generals were Sunni Muslims. They were descendants of Muhammad's adviser and his best student. Iraq is the only country that could keep Shite Muslim Iran in check. Iran is Shite, and they are descendants of Muhammad's cousin and son-in-law. The two religious fractions have been fighting each other for control of Islam since the year 632 AD when Muhammad died.

"Also, the Ba'ath Party Iraq generals knew America's history where we defeated Japan and let them keep their emperor and their government. This was in spite of the fact that Japan treated their American prisoners of war worse than any other country had ever treated them. Many Americans called for the death of their emperor, but he was allowed to live. The humane way we treated the Japanese and their emperor finalized their surrender and stopped the war.

"We had already proved how America deals with a vanquished nation and the Sunni generals believed, after Saddam Hussein was located, they would ultimately be in power.

"However, he hid for nine months. After he was finally captured, America didn't return power to the Sunni generals. A few months later the Sunni's began to chant anti-American slogans. Then the guerilla warfare started in earnest. It was part of the ongoing 1,300 year religious war between the Shite Muslims and the Sunni Muslims, and America was in the way.

"The argument for Americans to be there based on weapons of mass destruction no longer existed. I wanted to protect America, not fight for one Muslim sect against another Muslim sect. It was a war that would likely last another 1,300 years, but it was not my war. I had the time in rank and could retire, and I did."

"I am glad you retired," said Karen with a trace of sensuality in her smile. "Otherwise, I would never have met you. I'm going to keep the store and gun range and hope that this madness won't last. Are you going to join the Militia of One?"

"I'm not saying one way or the other. Secrecy is what gives the Militia power. But I will say that I fought a war for the freedoms we have in America and if necessary, I would fight again."

Karen nodded and said, "As you know, the military has been purged of patriotic generals and now has a command structure that is not loyal to our Constitution. They are only loyal to President Cramer. What will keep the generals from ordering the army to take over America? Do you think that the Marines will fight against the Militia of One?"

"No way. Most of them have friends and family members who own guns, and they will definitely not fight them. For example, I joined the Marines because my dad was a Marine. Also, every Marine learns that the 1878 Posse Comitatus Act prohibits the use of our military to enforce laws inside America.

"They also know the Bill of Rights guarantees that the people can keep and bear arms. All ten are about the rights of the people. And gun rights also protect the other nine. The one world government people, who want to control America, may really believe they will win. But at school we studied a lot of wars and found out that believing doesn't mean winning. The theoretical winner quite often lost.

"However, if the generals ask for volunteers and promise large bonuses, I can see a number of Marines and also army volunteers going. This could make for a very long war, and the Militia of One would not easily win. It also could be a terrible blood bath, possibly worse than the civil war where almost a million Americans died. It could last for many years."

The Gun War

"That's what I was afraid of," Karen said. "I probably won't be able to reopen my gun store. I am thinking that I can temporally reopen the store as a martial arts and knife facility. I have a good stash of money from selling those guns and ammo and not having to replace them. I heard that you had a lot of hand to hand martial art experience. Are you a black belt?"

"Kind of. For ten years I studied traditional Southern Shaolin Kung-Fu, Wu-Su. Unlike the modern Kung Fu and karate systems the old traditional Chinese Kung-Fu doesn't have colored belt. However, I would be equivalent to at least a third or fourth degree karate black belt."

"Would you be interested in being a martial arts and knife fighting instructor?"

"I would be pleased to teach martial art classes for you temporarily, or anything else you need. Give me a call and tell me when you want the classes to start."

"OK, I'll call you." Karen walked up to Hunter and gave him a hug that lasted way too long. It felt like a promise of things to come, and he really liked it.

Karen winked and walked away.

Chapter 5

State Times Post News, Digital Edition: Congressman Heckler and one of his bodyguards left his house for their early morning jog. Witnesses described a woman jogger suddenly getting up from a bench and running after them. She was fast and quickly closed the distance. She drew a gun from her fanny pack and within a few seconds both Heckler, and his bodyguard fell to the ground. She then fired a few more times into the Heckler's body and continued running until she disappeared from sight. Police are searching the area, but the witnesses' descriptions of the woman were very vague.

Dr. Birch arrived early for lunch in a private room of JJ's Lobster and Steak House. He sipped a glass of Bushmills Irish whiskey on the rocks as he waited for Craig to arrive. When he came in Dr. Birch stood and shook Craig's hand and motioned for him to sit to his left.

"They have great food here," said Dr. Birch. "I recommend their parcel of salmon with lobster, and they also have a great house salad."

"Well, I'm a steak and potato man, and I don't eat vegetables or salads," replied Craig. "I think I'll try their grilled filet mignon with Stilton Cream sauce."

"You never eat vegetables or salads?"

"No, I never liked them. Even when I was a kid, I didn't like them."

"Maybe that's why," Dr. Birch retorted with an unusually sarcastic tone.

Craig looked quizzically at the doctor and asked, "What do you mean by why?"

"Oh, nothing." Dr. Birch always wondered about people who didn't eat vegetables and thought that healthy food and proper nutrition were unimportant. He believed that good nutrition was essential for good health.

They ordered their food, and Dr. Birch glanced at the door to the private dining room to make sure it was closed. Satisfied there was no one listening, he asked Craig if he had read the short brochure.

"Yes, but what does it have to do with me?"

"World government in the guise of the United Nations is in the process of taking over America. Naturally, they want to disarm us so that there is minimal resistance to their eventual takeover. The fastest way to do this is to terrorize us with examples of innocent people, like my son. His wife said there were no guns in the house, and the agents pretended they had found a Smith & Wesson 38 special revolver in the closet. She said it was not their gun. The agents had planted it. America has turned into Nazi Germany.

"They killed him and thousands of other innocent civilians as their example of what will happen to anyone who doesn't turn in their guns. Our government has turned into a terrorist group with the goal of taking over our country and ending the need for free elections."

Just as Craig had feared, Dr. Birch was still harping on his son. Craig couldn't help but be sympathetic for the doctor having lost his only son, but he wondered if the doctor had forgotten about his little issue—incurable cancer. Hoping to deflect the topic for good, Craig answered, "Well, a few dangerous crazies in government, I guess."

"Please," Dr. Birch replied with a visibly annoyed tone as his face scrunched up like he had smelled something bad. He shook his head, took a long swig of his Irish whiskey and said, "It's a lot more complicated than that."

Coming to grips with the fact the doctor wasn't going to let this topic go and that he might as well enjoy an otherwise good lunch, Craig gave up and asked, "Well, President Cramer and the Supreme Court said the United Nations law is now the law of the land. What can anyone do except obey it?"

"Yes, he said that, but all laws take their legitimized form from our constitution and its amendments. The Second Amendment says they cannot infringe on our right to have guns. They cannot take our guns and pretend they still follow the Constitution. Many top government officials are breaking the law and must be eliminated."

Craig finally had enough. He stopped Dr. Birch in mid-thought and demanded, "Okay, Doctor, listen. In case you have forgotten, I'm here because I'm dying of cancer. I appreciate your situation with your son and am, indeed, truly sorry. I only want to know what's going to happen with my cancer. Can we stay focused here?"

Dr. Birch remained calm, not even slightly taken aback by Craig's uncharacteristic outburst. He understood Craig's apprehension concerning his condition. On many levels, he even counted on it.

Dr. Birch reassured him, "Craig, I know these conversations have been a little unorthodox..."

"Unorthodox?" Craig sarcastically countered.

"Unorthodox. But, while I thank you for your indulgence on this point, I have to assure you that this ties in with your situation right now. I ask you to bear with me for another two or three more minutes, because this topic, believe it or not, may very well change your life and, perhaps more importantly, the lives of your family."

Craig gave Dr. Birch a frustrated look, sat back in his chair and acquiesced. "Alright. I'll give you your three minutes to make this relevant to me. After that, I leave and find another doctor."

"Fair enough, I will get to the point. If you help me eliminate some of those murdering, law breaking politicians who ordered the death of my son, I will give you and your family one million dollars."

Craig was stunned and just sat there with his mouth open and multiple feelings whirling through his mind. Finally, he asked, "What do you mean? What do I have to do for that million dollars?"

"I will see that you and your wife and kids get one million dollars. That will easily pay off your home mortgage, your credit cards, and still have plenty of money to see your children through college and your wife through her old age."

A sickening feeling engulfed Craig's stomach. "What's the catch?"

"I'll give you one million dollars in American gold eagle coins, no records, no income tax. I have had the coins for many years so there are no longer any records of me buying them. And there will be no records of you receiving them. All you have to do is a bit of easy work with the pills your company provides its customers. If you agree, your work will be worth one million dollars."

"OK but very specifically, explain exactly what I have to do."

"You will compare a list of government officials against a list of your prescription pill customers in the Washington D. C. area. You will give me three pills from one prescription for each person on both lists. I will insert a poison inside one of the pills you give me. I have practiced and I can do this without a trace. I will do the hard work. All you have to do is pretend you are recounting the pills and put one poisoned pill in the top of the bottle so that it will be swallowed sooner rather that later. Wear gloves to be sure your fingerprints aren't on the bottle. And that's it. Make your rounds of the five stores you manage at a time when they are usually not busy."

"What kind of poison will you use?"

"Abrus precatorius, sometimes called the rosary pea, is a plant that grows wild in Florida. I have acquired a good supply of the seeds. Then I refined the abrin poison from the seeds. It is one of the most potent toxins known to man. A dose of only 0.1 mg, basically the size of a small dot, will cause multiple organ system failure. It is fatal in two or three days. I will use one hundred times the fatal dose. There is no known antidote, and it is always fatal."

With wide eyes, a clenched jaw over this shocking news, and imagining the worst possible outcome, Craig managed to ask, "Could I get caught?"

"Not really. As long as you keep your mouth shut, it's pretty much foolproof. The pill or capsule will look exactly like the rest. Since there is only one pill, and the rest of the pills are normal, the evidence will disappear before an investigation begins. It will have already dissolved prior to any medical examination.

"The initial manifestation of ingested abrin poisoning resembles food poisoning or infectious gastroenteritis. It will be assumed it was in some food that was eaten or something injected. There will be no evidence left behind, and a typical investigator won't find anything. Even if they do find that he was poisoned, they will have no idea how.

"You did not fill the prescription. You don't even like guns, so there is no motive. They won't know you received the untraceable gold, and even if they do find it, you may have been saving gold coins most of your life. If you are ever questioned, just act like you don't know what the heck they are talking about. There will be no proof that will hold up in a court of law."

"But murdering people isn't right. How do I live with that?"

"First of all, killing is not the same as murdering. Killing is not illegal and it is normal in war. Killing, unlike murder, is not a crime. Murdering is the illegal taking of life, but killing in war is perfectly legal. We are now in a war. Also, killing is morally sanctioned when you are enslaved and fight to be free.

"The current government has turned into a terrorist organization, sending their goons to innocent people's homes and murdering them simply because they own a gun. By helping to rid us of this government you will be saving many thousands of lives that would be lost in the coming revolution.

"Throughout history untold millions of people have killed and died for the cause of freedom and liberty. Most of America's heroes have either killed or ordered people killed. Our military was created with the purpose of killing people.

"You will be doing something for your family and for your country. Fate has chosen you for this great mission." Dr. Birch smiled. "This is your moment, your destiny. You can turn your negative final year into a positive victory for yourself, your family and for free people everywhere. You have an opportunity to literally change the world for the better. You can help make the world a safer place.

Your children will live in a much better world than the one either of us know."

Craig nervously asked, "Many of the Congressmen probably get their drugs in the mail. Also, we are not the only drug store chain in town. What if there are only a few of them that do business with my stores?"

"Let me worry about that. I am betting that there will be between ten and thirty targets. But I guarantee I will pay you by the job, and not the number of targets. So I will pay you even if there are only five or ten. What do you say?"

Craig sat in silence for almost a minute and knew that Dr. Birch was waiting for an answer. He cleared his throat and swallowed hard so that he could speak. "Dr. Birch, I hate to disappoint you, but I'm no James Bond or anything like that." He swallowed again and wiped at his mouth. Lowering his voice to a whisper, he asked, "Is this for real? Are you serious, messing with me, crazy, or all of the above?"

"Pardon my pun, but I'm deadly serious. And I need your answer now or the deal's off, and I will easily find someone else. You know that your pharmacy is not the only one in town."

"American was conceived in a revolution against a powerful government, and our Constitution is against powerful government; the Constitution is for freedom of the individual. The only way to protect our freedom is through another revolution.

"You have an opportunity to literally change the world for the better. You can help make the world a safer place," Dr. Birch said with a thoughtful smile. "You will have the knowledge that you changed history. But you have to decide now." Dr. Birch saw an overwhelmed look of bewilderment in Craig's eyes.

Craig had to make the toughest decision of his life. His decision was not about which college to go to, or whether he should join the Air Force or the Navy. The decision didn't even compare to which girl to marry. For Craig, this was a decision about taking part in the Militia of One revolution, which he didn't understand. And he would be taking the lives of people he had never even met. There could never be a harder decision.

Craig knew that he was dying. He knew that death was the unavoidable path of every human life. But that didn't make the decision any easier.

Craig had never given much thought to the greater questions of life and death. But now the age old questions of what life was and why he was alive invaded his mind. It wasn't really that Craig loved life that much. It was more the fear of the unknown of death.

The guilt he felt in his failure as a husband and father tipped the scale. It reduced his once high self-esteem, and now he felt inadequate. This was an opportunity to do one final but necessary thing for his family.

Just when he thought he had decided, his mind flip-flopped again. A war raged in his head, the forces of caring for his family on one side and the poisoning of strangers on the other.

The Gun War

Then there was the money. Craig had no stock portfolio to leave his wife. The house had a second mortgage, and his life insurance was not enough to pay it off. Craig knew the family's dire financial situation was entirely his fault. He made good money as a district pharmacy manager, but he couldn't hang on to that money. It seemed to slip through his fingers. He couldn't even pay off his medical bills and his Visa card every month. If Craig didn't take Dr. Birch's offer, his family would really suffer, and it would be his fault.

Time was running out, and Dr. Birch wanted an answer now.

"Will you do it or not? I need to know now."

"Okay, okay, I'll do it."

"You made the right choice. Remember the prime directive in this operation is silence. So please, don't ever tell anyone, not even your wife. For obvious reasons, this must be kept a complete and very deep secret!"

"I won't, don't worry." Craig stood and shook hands with Dr. Birch. He had hardly touched his food but left in a daze, closing the door behind him. Sitting in his car, he thought that he could always back out but no use upsetting Dr. Birch yet.

Chapter 6

State Times Post News, Digital Edition: President Sam Cramer said, "America's new treaty with the United Nations will make the whole world safer. Disobedience to the United Nations treaty means immediate internment in temporary camps and re-educated to gain a new appreciation of law. Anyone who uses violence to protest this historic life saving treaty will face swift military justice and execution."

Representative Gutenberg, the Speaker of the House, was one of the most strident gun grabbers in America. He had encouraged his friends in the Senate to ratify the United Nations Treaty that began this government terrorism. Patrick decided that his elimination would send a loud message to the Hill. But a good gorilla fighter never undertakes a mission without a well thought out plan, and that includes a good getaway strategy. Hunter was his mentor back in their Marine days, so Patrick knew he could ask him for help.

Patrick slapped a magnetic sign on to the side of his van that read: "Communication Contractor." It also listed the company's name and phone number. This would help alleviate any fears from any curious or suspicious neighbors while he parked near their house. The phone number was from a throw away phone that Patrick had with him and could answer if someone called to verify that the vehicle was authentic.

He positioned a miniature surveillance recording video camera on a telephone pole that would provide a good view of Gutenberg's house and his comings and goings. It had an extended battery and took a picture every thirty seconds. Each picture had a time stamp on it so the details of the surveillance would make sense. After a week Patrick retrieved the camera. It showed that a black SUV picked up Gutenberg every weekday morning between 6:10 and 6:20. The bodyguard would come out of the house and look around. Then Gutenberg would come out and they'd get in the SUV. During the workweek, the procedure went like clockwork. At that early hour, there was only the SUV; no other cars were driving down the street.

Patrick met Hunter for breakfast at Honeybee's and they got a private booth in the back. "Hunter, as you requested, I've been surveying the Speaker's house for a week."

"Good. Which rifle did you decide on using?"

"My grandfather gave me a World War II Russian sniper rifle when I was fifteen years old. It's a 7.62 mm Mosin-Nagant M91/30 with a PU sniper scope. The Russians used these as sniper rifles during the war. They were very accurate against the Germans. I can consistently shoot a four inch group at two blocks, so one block is a snap."

"That's better than good. I will get you a vehicle. Toss your gun and an escape bag in it, and tomorrow morning, park at the corner of the street near Gutenberg's house. Shoot from inside your car so your brass stays in the car, and you can immediately drive off on your escape route to rendezvous with me."

"What kind of vehicle will you get?"

"I'm not sure. I will go to my exercise club where those trusting people usually put their car keys in an unguarded cubbyhole. I will take a key, see which car it beeps and drive away. Then I will turn on my jammer that fools a GPS receiver into thinking the satellites are not available."

"Why do you need a jammer?"

Most cars nowadays are equipped with telematics systems. These have two-way links to service providers that relay GPS data. This gives the authorities the ability to see where the car is and remotely disable it. When I get the car back to my garage, I will disable that system and attach a new license plate on it and bring it to you."

"Will it be a stolen plate?"

"Not really. I snapped a photo of a license plate of some random car parked in the mall, and printed it out. Then I attached it to a thin board and sprayed it with some clear glossy paint in case it rains and put it in a frame. It looks perfect and I will tape it over the existing plate of whatever vehicle I end up with. So your car will have a license that is not hot and no one will be looking for it. Make sure to wear gloves so you don't leave prints."

"Wow. Where did you learn all that?"

"A friend was telling me a story of some high school kids who were upset that their small town's new Traffic Camera Program was giving them tickets for running through red lights even though they came to a complete stop before turning right. For revenge the students took a picture of the mayor's license plate. They printed it out and taped it over theirs. Then, early the next morning, they went around the block at least fifty times. A week later the Mayor received over fifty tickets in the mail."

"What did the Mayor do after that?"

Hunter ignored the question. "Wear a hat with a large brim and big sunglasses to throw off any traffic cameras that might snap your picture as you drive by. And leave your smart phone at home, they're always being tracked. I have a few untraceable throwaway phones; here is one that you can use if you need to call me. Leave it in this metal can until you need to use it."

"Why the metal can?"

"It is like a Faraday cage and blocks radio signals. This way there is no record of where the phone is until you need to use it. After you use it put it back in the can. There is one more thing. Did you find a good spot to switch cars?"

"Yes, it's right here on the map. There is a small parking lot hidden from the road at the back of a strip mall. There are no cameras there, and it is empty in the early morning. You can wait for me there."

"OK. When the job is done leave the key in the ignition. Also, put the window down so eventually some local thug will see the key and likely steal the car. I will be waiting at our rendezvous location in my car. Put your rifle, spent brass and the fake license plate in the garment bag I've brought today and bring it to my car. I will drive you back to my place, and you'll take your own car and go to work. You could be slightly late, but tell them you had a flat. It will be a good alibi if there are any problems. Any last minute questions?"

"Yeah, that's some great planning. What kind of training did you have before I met you in Iraq?"

"Patrick, I can't talk about that, but I was well trained. Anything else?"

"I noticed you were getting friendly with Karen. She's a beautiful girl, pretty well built, a lot of curves in the right places, and she has a great smile. Are you going to make a move on her?"

"I have never had to split the blanket and unlike you divorced guys, I still have all my own stuff. So I'm in no hurry and my only answer is she is just a friend for now. We'll have to see how I feel about her later."

Hunter liked Patrick even though they were a lot different. Patrick was much smaller and weaker than Hunter and didn't like direct conflicts. He preferred to do his fighting anonymously and often from a position of stealth. Hunter on the other hand often charged ahead and challenged everyone in his path. But when necessary he could also use stealth. But challenging the wrong people, instead of being an automatic "yes sir" type of person was probably the reason he never was promoted beyond the rank of major.

The Gun War

"Patrick, one thing I always liked about you is that you were kind of the Radar Riley of our Marine Battalion. Remember the time I asked you to set up a party for our team and you really came through with everything we needed. They talked for months about the time when you illegally borrowed a two and a half ton truck from the motor pool. You were able to trade a scrounged load of lumber for fifty cases of beer we needed for our party. There was a rumor that you almost got caught. Tell me what happened there."

"I successfully returned the truck to the motor pool and went to hang up the keys when a jeep with one star on the front pulled up and the brigadier general got out and said, 'Son, you didn't steal that truck, did you?'

"I saluted and immediately answered with the first thing that came to my mind. 'No sir. I constructively co-located it.' Those words really don't mean anything but the general, not wanting to appear dumb in front of a mere young sergeant, hesitated a second and then said, 'OK. Carry on, son.'"

Hunter smiled and said, "That was really quick thinking, and I remember that it was a wonderful party, but there is a question I always wanted to ask you. Remember the time that Captain Bob Peterson turned in his readiness report to General Boren, and it was filled with many expressions of fucking. He claimed someone had messed with his computer, but upon close inspection no one could find anything wrong with his computer. Now that we're both retired you can tell me. Was that you who in some way caused Peterson's problem?"

Patrick's eyes brightened. "Yeah, that was me alright. Peterson had a bad attitude. He didn't approve of my personality and was being quite difficult so I wrote a simple little computer subroutine that used the find and replace command to look for the word "the" and replaced it with 'the fucking'. But it only showed up when the document went through the printing process.

"He was writing an important readiness report for the general. Everything looked great on his computer screen, but when he sent it over to the printer the simple little find and replace subroutine made the changes on the printed page. Peterson was in a hurry and, like most people, he didn't read the printed page since he had already checked it on the screen. But when the general and other people in the meeting read it, they were not amused. The general didn't believe Peterson didn't know about it. He thought that Peterson had a bad attitude and treated him accordingly.

"As you know, Peterson retired a half a year after the incident. I think he figured that he was no longer on the fast track for promotion. And he was damn right.

"I didn't actually mean to force him to retire. I only wanted to get him off my back. Fortunately, my subroutine was set to only work for one document. Then it automatically erased itself, leaving no evidence behind. So when Peterson's computer was inspected by the Information Technology people, nothing was found. That helped make Peterson look guilty. He was much nicer to me and to everyone when he saw how his bad attitude could come back and really bite him. Yes, even back then I was a computer geek, and he suspected me. But there was absolutely no proof. And just because you know your way around computers doesn't make you guilty."

"Good story. I'll get the car and stuff you might need and see you at my house tomorrow at five in the morning."

"I'll be there."

Chapter 7

State Times Post News, Digital Edition: Justice Fleming, an anti-gun member of the Ninth Circuit Court, died after digesting arsenic trioxide poison. This form of arsenic dissolves readily in water and is colorless and tasteless.

Justice Fleming had a wife and several mistresses so there are numerous suspects. The investigation has just begun and police have not eliminated anyone including Militia of One sympathizers. The ancient Greeks and Romans knew about arsenic and during the nineteenth century it was widely use in various murders.

"Hey, Patrick, right on time. Park you car in my garage. Your new ride is the car next to it. I put in a garment bag to disguise your rifle and also a small bag filled with various emergency escape equipment."

"What's in the escape bag?"

"A throw away cell phone in a metal can that I told you about. Also there's an untraceable 1911 pistol loaded with extreme penetrator ammo. I included a 9 ounce container of maximum strength capsaicin bear pepper spray that is big and powerful enough to stop a charging bear, extra latex gloves and a few other things you will probably never need."

The Gun War

"Wow, you found me a fifty thousand dollar Mercedes-Benz E-Class sedan. This ought to be plenty fast enough for me. I'm ready. Let's do it."

At 5:20 AM Patrick parked in a no parking to corner zone on a side street approximately a block from the target. This manicured and affluent suburb of Washington D. C. had rows of tastefully decorated upscale homes. Cast-iron street lampposts lined both sides of the street. As the morning light from the new day arrived the streetlights automatically turned off.

Last week, as a test, when Patrick parked in this neighborhood at 6:00 AM, not a soul stirred. And except for a barking dog a half block away, this morning was no different.

Patrick was relaxed as he waited for the target's regular ride to the office to drive up. He watched with keen focused eyes, very much like warriors and hunters have done throughout human history. His breathing was slow, and he relaxed and cleared his mind. All was quiet, and he concentrated on his upcoming task.

Patrick slowly put his hand outside the car and estimated the cross wind to be no more than eight miles an hour. He adjusted his riflescope to compensate for the very slight deviation the mild wind would cause. He watched and patiently waited. Patrick checked his watch. 6:10. The Speaker should come out any moment now.

Right on time the black limo arrived, parked and the driver got out. The target's bodyguard opened the house door and looked around. Patrick rolled down his passenger side window just enough to make the shot and took aim. Satisfied that there was no observable threat, the bodyguard motioned with his hand. House Speaker Gutenberg came out and started towards the limo.

Patrick knew that the muzzle velocity of his hand loaded 7.62 mm round from this particular rifle was almost 2,600 feet per second. Even though the bullet would create a sonic boom, he knew the target would not hear anything until the bullet struck because the speed of sound is only 1,126 feet per second. The bullet would get there before the sound.

At the bullet's supersonic speed it would only take a third of a second from his location for the bullet to the travel to the target. You can't walk very far in a third of a second. So it was quite possible to hit a walking target. Still he preferred to shoot a stationary target instead of a walking target. So he decided to use the second of relative slowness when the target stopped to stoop down and get into the back seat of the car.

Patrick's Marine rifle training kicked in. He took a deep breath and let it out slowly. Then he very gently squeezed the trigger, tighter and tighter. The gun fired with an impressive flash. Even with his earplugs, the sound inside the vehicle was deafening and Patrick immediately saw the target fall. Patrick grinned in the pride of a job well done. With a ringing in his ears, he started his engine. Trying to be stealth and not attract undue attention, he slowly pulled out of his parking place. Once around the next corner he floored it and kept one eye on his review mirror. Hunter will be proud of me, he thought as he continued to accelerate and complete his getaway.

Then for a long moment he froze in bewilderment. He saw a black Ford police interceptor sedan pulling out and burning rubber as it raced towards him. *Damn, damn it!* he thought. *Bad luck.* There was some kind of unexpected chase car on his tail. Where could it have come from? Gut-wrenching fear took over and he gunned his car.

Fortunately, Patrick had a fast car and it was very early, well before rush hour, and there was almost no traffic. He moved his hands up on the wheel, got a firmer grip, swallowed hard and stomped the accelerator. Patrick took the first right and stepped on it. Then he took a left and hooked another left. The sensation of streets and moving cars flooded his brain almost too quickly to process.

After the last turn, Patrick thought he had lost the chase car. But suddenly it was still there and gaining. Another right, then a right and through a red light, but it was still closing. The chase car was quickly gaining ground. Now it was only five car lengths behind him. He began to panic. He rolled down his window and grabbed the can of bear spray from his escape bag. He had a tight feeling round his chest and an empty feeling in the pit of his stomach. His heartbeat was racing as he held the bear spray can out the window and sprayed till it was empty.

Patrick was relieved as he saw the chase car fell back. Patrick took a right and then blew through the next stop sign, but there it was again, that same car, and it was closing fast.

Now Patrick was really scared. He began to sweat profusely but tried to take slow, deep breaths to stay calm. It didn't work. His whole body was literally shaking and hundreds of thoughts whirled through his brain.

He reached into his escape bag again and touched the 1911 45-caliber pistol. He was well trained in its use, and it gave him some momentary comfort. The chase car was now so close it hit the back of his bumper, causing his car to swerve slightly clockwise, however Patrick was able to recover control and his car raced ahead.

It was happening so fast and he knew that it was time for plan B, and there was no plan C except maybe to shoot it out with the chase car or call Hunter, who was in the neighborhood waiting for him.

Patrick pulled out a handful of caltrops. These are hollow four prong spikes and no matter how they land, there is always one spike pointing upward. They are used to puncture either regular or self-healing tires and quickly deflate them. He tossed them over the roof of his car and they landed in the street.

Patrick looked in his review mirror, straining to see signs that the chase car had a blow out or was slowing down. No such luck.

The Gun War

Patrick swore whiskey tango foxtrot under his breath as the black car kept closing with him. He threw out another handful of caltrops, but the chase car kept coming. Then the chase car hit his bumper again. This time it was damn hard, and Patrick knew there would be a lot of damage. His trembling hands tightly gripped the steering wheel in dreaded anticipation of another bump. His pulse was pounding, and sweat was dripping down his head and into his eyes. His only hope was that his car was still intact and would hold together and keep driving fast. Somehow he would get away. He had to get away.

Then, to his surprise, the chase car started falling back. Patrick gained a bigger lead, and in his review mirror it looked like one of their front tires was beginning to get very soft, affecting the cars handling. Relieved and emotionally drained, he yelled loudly to no one in particular. Tears of joy rolled down his face. It felt great, and he turned another corner and lost the chase car completely.

Two miles and a few turns later he pulled behind the strip mall where Hunter was waiting. The mall didn't open until ten so this early no one was around. Patrick threw everything in his bag while Hunter yanked off the fake license plate.

"Remember to leave the key in the ignition and roll down the window."

"Sorry. I'll get to it now."

One minute later they pulled out in Hunter's car. Hunter noticed that Patrick was covered in sweat and his hands were still shaking. "From the looks of the back of the car I obtained for you, there must have been some unexpected trouble."

"Yea, it was literally touch and go for a few minutes there."

"Did you complete the job?"

"The target fell down. I am not sure if Speaker Gutenberg is alive or dead, but he was hit."

"Great. The main thing is that you hit him. Whether he lives or dies is immaterial to our cause. When they decreed that our guns were now illegal, the people realized that the politicians were the ones who were illegal. Alive or dead, your shot will install fear in the political elite class. They don't mind sending us to fight their wars. But they sure as hell don't want to fight a war themselves. But now they have to."

"I understand exactly."

Patrick had seen some combat in Iraq, and he was fine. But now, even after the incident was over, his body was still trembling. He hoped it would go away quickly and Hunter would not notice.

Hunter grinned and said, "Running for you life on the streets is a lot different than engaging in an Iraq fire fight. But you did good." Patrick just nodded.

Back in Hunter's garage Hunter said, "I see you're still a bit sweaty from the chase. But otherwise you look fine. You can drive to the air force base and work will be your alibi. But I don't believe you will ever need one. I know you have some kind of civil service job at Jefferson Air Force

Base Golf Course, but what exactly do you do there?"

"I supervise the ground crew, and it's a really cushy job."

Hunter turned to look at Patrick intently and asked, "That's where President Cramer plays golf sometimes, isn't it?"

"Yes. He likes their course, and it is fairly close to the White House. And most important, it is very secure. He's there almost every week. For a couple of hours, no one but President Cramer and his party and of course tons of the secret service agents can be on the course."

"That gives me an idea."

"I'm not sure what you're thinking, but President Cramer is very well protected there. The Secret Service doesn't just have a few agents there. They are out in force and they check absolutely everything. There are at least fifty Secret Service bodyguards and they look like they are impossible to penetrate.

"No other groups are even allowed to play golf when Cramer is there. No planes fly overhead. No one is allowed anywhere near the President. And that includes the employees such as me. I have to go indoors and wait until they are finished.

"It's only a thought, but there might be some way. Well, better get to work and I will talk to you later. And by the way, great job today!"

"Thanks."

"Leave the rifle in my car and I will safely dispose of it. Also, leave the flash drive from your surveillance camera. I want to check it to see where they were parking that chase car in the past weeks."

After Patrick left, Hunter completely disassembled the rifle, wiped it down, and smashed the barrel flat with a heavy sledgehammer. He then took the pieces, wrapped them in dirty bags and put them in various commercial trash bins around the neighborhood.

The Gun War

Chapter 8

State Times Post News, Digital Edition: General Redstone, Chairman of the Joint Chiefs of Staff, said, "Our military officers and enlisted men understand that they have sworn to uphold the Constitution of the United States of America. They have not sworn to uphold the Supreme Court's obviously mistaken interpretation of it."

"They know that our Bill of Rights is part of the Constitution, and it supersedes everything in the Constitution. It is obvious that United Nation's law is not higher law than America's Bill of Rights. Any other interpretation would mean that America has turned into a third world lawless nation."

"The Joint Chiefs of Staff stands with the Constitution and asks all personnel under its command not to become involved with either side in America's gun issues. The military will not enforce martial law in violation of the Posse Comitatus Act."

Craig was happy that the first part of his work was over. But the remaining part would be the hardest. He arrived at Dr. Birch's office at the end of the day when everyone else was gone.

"Hi, Craig. Excellent work. I have altered one pill for each of the thirteen targets you uncovered. There is no sign they have been tampered with. I disposed of all the lab material, so there is absolutely no evidence left behind. Here are the pills, each in this small envelope with your code name for the target.

"Since you already have the automatic refill dates, all you have to do is wait for the date, visit the store for a quantity accuracy check, and slip in the altered pill. Make sure to put it on top so that it is more likely it will be swallowed sooner rather than later."

"Also be sure to wear gloves when you touch the pill bottles. And as an extra safety precaution, be out of range of any cameras."

"No problem there. I always gloves when counting pills. Slipping in one pill will go completely unnoticed. When will I get paid?"

"After a few of the thirteen are actually eliminated. But as soon as you have slipped in the last pill, put in your retirement papers for health reasons. I already have the gold coins in my bank box. So I will get them to you, and you can take them to your bank box or wherever you choose."

"Sounds like a plan. But won't you feel guilty in murdering those people just to revenge your son?"

"First of all, as I already said, killing an enemy during a war is not murder. Murder is defined as the unlawfully taking of life. Killing an enemy during a declared war is completely lawful. We will legally win this war.

"Second, it is only partially revenge. Sure, it started out as revenge, but now it is about saving America from dictatorship. With a swift victory I will have saved many lives and made sure this never happens to anyone else's son."

"And third, if the Second Amendment is not legal then nothing in the Constitution is legal. And since all American laws come from the power of the Constitution, then there are no legal laws. The fact is that we now live in a state of anarchy.

"I really struggled with getting over my son's murder. But my minister said that God knew I could handle my son's murder. This is my way of handling it. And as for killing those murderers, I will still sleep like a baby."

"OK, OK I will do my part," said Craig. "Putting one pill in a bottle is child's play, and since I am the supervisor, nothing can go wrong. That's why I agreed. No one will say a word to me for checking the count of a prescription bottle. I have done it many times before. After all, every one of my company's Washington pharmacies reports to me. Hopefully, there will be no problems."

The Gun War

Chapter 9

State Times Post News, Digital Edition: President Charmer said, "There appears to be a backlash by a few criminal types against our life protecting universal gun regulations. They will absolutely fail, but currently they have created a bit of anxiety among some lawmakers. There is no doubt that these few criminals will be quickly caught and brought to justice.

Another executive order by President Cramer stated that the owners and executives of any news media who said anything favorable concerning the terrorist Militia of One criminals would be arrested and jailed as enemies of the people.

Senator Eberstadt was strongly against gun ownership. He was up for reelection this year but so far his polls showed him losing by over ten percent. His campaign manager had arranged numerous speeches in an attempt to reverse the polls, emphasizing the senator's efforts in getting perks for his constitutions and avoiding any mention of gun control.

Mindful of the current dangers Eberstadt hired extra bodyguards and will give his political speech from behind a bulletproof speakers podium and bulletproof glass. And additional precautions have surely been taken. The government will reimburse the cost, so expensive safety precautions were ordered.

Patrick Sullivan moved slowly towards the stage until he was twenty yards from the podium. The hard part was waiting for Senator Eberstadt to begin speaking.

Right on time, the senator was escorted by his body guards on to the elevated outdoor stage. The crowd of over three thousand voters settled down. Senator Eberstadt put a fake warm smile on his face and began talking. It was a feel good speech and the crowd periodically erupted to applause when the senator told them what they wanted to hear.

Patrick pretended to listen to the speech as he silently rehearsed his plan of attack. He expected that Senator Eberstadt would have bulletproof protection in front of him but there would be no protection behind him. And that is the way it looked.

His plan was to toss a M67 hand grenade over the podium and hopefully that would eliminate any collateral damage to the crowd of people. Since the stage was ten feet high, and the grenade has an effective casualty radius of up to 16 yards on flat ground, theoretically everything would work out.

Patrick was his high school's baseball pitcher, and had he thrown hundreds of grenades in practice and war. After the rifle, the grenade was his weapon of choice. He held the grenade upright with the pull ring away from the palm of his throwing hand so that the pull ring could be easily removed by his free hand.

When the next applause moment began he began his attack. Taking a deep breath, he pulled out the grenade pin with his index finger. Waiting a few seconds to calm his mind he looked at the target.

When Patrick felt he was ready, in one quick movement he tossed the grenade over the podium towards the back of the stage where it would only eliminate those on the stage. Then, just as fast, he ducked down as if to tie his shoe. Seconds later there was a deafening explosion and everyone froze as if time had stopped.

Panic erupted in the crowd as they began running away from the stage. Patrick stood and quickly joined the crowd in their mad dash to find safety. Some people were screaming and everyone was trying to get away from the perceived danger. It became a helter skelter stampede to get away from the explosion.

Thirty yards into his escape, a uniformed cop suddenly stopped him. He took out his gun, and said, "I saw that. You are under arrest."

The cop was so close Patrick could smell his astringent aftershave. But all he felt was fear. A pointed gun speaks with a language that is understood by people everywhere, and Patrick froze and raised his hands. He felt his nervous breathing accelerate and his heartbeat speed up.

The Gun War

Chapter 10

State Times Post News, Digital Edition: Stanford Burgess was shot to death while trying to escape from the Russell Senate Office Building. Cameras show that when entering, his wooden cane easily passed through the metal detector. The cane was then altered and three sharp metal blades were placed in slots and super glued into the tip of the cane. Officials suspected that the blades were hidden in Burgess's cell phone. Burgess entered the restroom to glue the blades onto the tip of the cane and change it into a deadly weapon.

An hour later, witnesses state that Burgess used his improvised weapon as a spear that sliced through the right side of the Senator Brubeck's neck, cutting his carotid artery.

While trying to escape he used an emergency fire exit door. The police said there was a loaded gun hidden outside near the emergency door. The alarm sounded, and Burgess shot and killed a security guard before being shot by a second security guard. The incident is still under investigation.

Suddenly, seemingly out of nowhere, Hunter mysteriously appeared. He saw the fear in Patrick's facial expression. The policeman's gun was still pointed directly at Patrick's chest.

Patrick's hand grenade idea had problems, Hunter thought, but he knew he had to save his gunny. It is the Marine code. Feelings about protecting your people on the battlefield are ingrained in you and you can't change them. Hunter smiled. He was calm and said to the cop, "It's not him. He was with me."

The cop then pointed his gun at Hunter and said, "Then you freeze too. You're both under arrest."

Hunter knew that the subconscious part of a human mind could simultaneously think about millions of things at the same time. And it reacts very quickly and instinctively. By contrast the conscious logical part of the mind can only think of one thing at the exact same moment. So it reacts much slower that the subconscious. The task for Hunter was to take this cop out of his subconscious fighting mind and put him in his conscious mind with a reassuring question.

Hunter smiled at the cop and said, "You win— you win. What do you want?" When a gun is pointed at you, slowing down the trigger finger by a second, or even by a fraction of a second, is very important. Hunter knew he couldn't hesitate from doing what he needed to do.

That reassuring but completely atypical answer and question required a logical answer from the cop's conscious part of his brain.

The cop's logical thought process brought him from his aggressive fight of flight subconscious mind back into his slower logical conscious mind.

For a brief moment, the cop paused. His eyes widened, and he opened his mouth to start to say something. As soon as the cop opened his mouth Hunter exploded into action.

It happened so rapidly and so unexpectedly that it was a total surprise to the cop. Hunter's entire being was controlled by automatic reflexes that had been drilled into him by some of the most demanding training in the world. His eyes observed everything with total clarity, and the events seemed to happen in slow motion. Hunter went into his martial arts mode. His mind instinctively concentrated on the task at hand.

From below the cop's field of vision, Hunter's left hand came up and grabbed the cop's gun hand. Hunter moved the gun over to his right and away from him. At the same time, Hunter turned his body clockwise to remove his body from the direction of the gun. As he did this, his right leg stepped backwards to further remove his body from the gun. These three simultaneous movements pointed the gun away from Hunter and moved Hunter's body even further from the direction where the gun was aimed.

Hunter quickly brought his right hand to the gun. Hunter's movements continued to flow from his years of training. His right hand grabbed the barrel of the gun.

Hunter now had his two strong hands on the gun and was in complete control. He forced the gun back towards the head of the cop. The barrel was now pointed towards the cop. If the gun went off now, it would not hit Hunter or Patrick.

The Gun War

The cop tried to draw his hand back, but the cop was not going to win. The gun was effectively neutralized, but Hunter continued the movement.

Hunter quickly repositioned his right foot behind the cop's right foot in preparation to slam him into the ground. At the same time Hunter rotated his torso putting pressure on the cop's hand. The movement then flowed into a right forearm smash to the cop's left temple.

Hunter completed his martial arts movement, and the cop fell to the ground. The cop fell hard in front of him, lengthwise, face up, motionless, and unconscious but without permanent injury.

The whole movement took less than two seconds, and Patrick just stood there frozen and with a shocked expression on his face. Wasting no time, Hunter grabbed Patrick and hustled him quickly in the direction of his car. Moving with the other spectators away from the stage, they successfully got to Hunter's car without any more interference.

Safely in, they drove, purposely slow, about four miles along a previously planned escape route before stopping and taking off the fake license plate and completing their escape.

Patrick glanced over at Hunter, expecting a look of anger or disapproval. But instead he saw a smile on Hunter's face. It wasn't a smile of satisfaction. Instead it was a smile of brotherhood, the knowledge that your Marine brothers always have each others' backs.

When Patrick calmed down he asked, "Wasn't that a very risky thing for you to do? Do you think you killed him?"

"No. When I noticed that the cop's trigger finger was in the safe position outside of the trigger guard position, I knew I had more time than usual for that move. And no, the cop will have a bad headache, but he will definitely survive. The escaping crowd was focused on running from the explosion. Any descriptions of us would likely be very inaccurate."

"How did you get there so quickly?"

"Are you complaining?"

"No, but you're completely unpredictable. I thought you would be in the car. How did you know I needed you?"

Hunter grinned but didn't answer.

Patrick became flustered by Hunter's strategic silence, but he knew that sometimes Hunter chose not to make small talk

The Gun War

Chapter 11

State Times Post News, Digital Edition: There is an urgent request for experienced bodyguards. Because of the recent troubles, some bodyguards have quit their jobs. Consequently, there is a huge demand for bodyguards, and there seems to be hardly any qualified people available for this position. President Cramer has agreed to make some of the Secret Service personnel available to protect key lawmakers. He said that these professionals could easily safeguard many of lawmakers who might be targets.

Now safely home, Hunter just shook his head and said, "That was exciting. But your grenade plan was way too risky. Fortunately, the end result was good but the risk was not.

"That was a good on target grenade throw, but you were easily caught. The idea is to get the job done and also minimize any risk to us or any innocent bystanders.

"In the future, I will plan the eliminations. Planning and organizing is what I was trained for. Are you okay with that?"

"You planned the sniper attack and that was very close to being a disaster," said Patrick.

"Patrick, the plan was good, but your execution was bad. Yes, I planned it, but you were supposed to case it and make sure it was feasible. I don't see how you missed seeing the second chase car before you took your shot. I think the only explanation is that you were so focused on the shot that you didn't pay attention to the car behind it. Your surveillance obviously has something to be desired."

"It never showed up on the surveillance camera and I didn't see it. I have no explanation."

"We are going to do my plan next. If we're taking turns, then it is my turn."

Exhausted, drained and knowing he screwed up with the grenade idea, Patrick just answered, "Yeah sure. Do you have a new plan?"

"Yes, it just so happens I do. From now on I will focus on very important targets that will make a real difference in this war. Also, I will plan operations that minimize our chances of getting caught.

"I am working on a few completely separate game changing plans. And your help with them is critical. These plans are not just going after a congressman. The plans have an extremely low probability of us getting caught. And they have a very high ability to seriously shake up the establishment. In fact, it is possible that this could end the gun war."

"Tell me," said Patrick.

"The plans are still taking shape, so I can't say anything quite yet. But it is not too early to get some of the more difficult hardware. I will need fifty pounds of C-4. Can you use your various Radar Riley connections to scrounge it from some Marine quartermaster you know?"

"If I have to use your name to get it, would that be alright?"

"No, don't do that. To minimize risk, I'd rather keep everything compartmentalized and as a need to know with absolutely no exceptions. That means with as few names as possible. Also, don't say what you need it for. If your supplier pushes you tell him that you have some big boulders on your land and you want to break them up.

"Remember that secrecy lies at the very heart of the Militia of One. Without it the anti-freedom, money-corrupted political establishment would quickly defeat us. Can you work on that tomorrow?"

"Definitely. Is there anything more you can tell me about the plan?"

"These projects could really make a big difference. I am not ready to say anything at this time. But get the C-4, and I will explain slightly more about the first plan."

"And if I can't?"

"If you can't get it, there are other avenues that I might be able to get it from. I will have to go to plan B or plan C or plan Z, but I will get what I need. Still, I know that you will do the very best you can to get it. You always seemed to come through and get everything we needed. It would sure be an easier solution that my next best method."

"Yeah, you're right. I'm going to work now and get an alibi for today, but I will get on your new project first thing tomorrow. And I've procured a lot more difficult things. So I don't expect any problems with the C-4."

"One more thing. Are you still the manager of ground keeping at Jefferson Air Force Base?"

"Yes, it's a great job. I just supervise the work, and I'm good at it. The top management really likes me."

"Great. Let me know as soon as you locate the C-4. This could be an explosion heard around the world. But we only have so much time to get everything together."

Chapter 12

State Times Post News, Digital Edition: United Nations Secretary General Mohammed Hussein has died. He had been sick for a few days and tests show he suffered from Thallium poisoning. It is unknown where the poison came from since none was found in his house.

Thallium is located between mercury and lead on the periodic table and is a very poisonous heavy metal. It was once used as a rat poison, but was discontented due to some cases of human poisoning. There are also a number of old cases where it was used in political assassinations.

Craig glanced at a magazine while waiting to see his doctor, but he wasn't really reading. He felt more depressed and lethargic than usual, and his recent slouching posture caused his neck and back to hurt.

The waiting room was now getting on his last nerve. He didn't like those glaring LED ceiling lights and the pastel blue paint job that was supposed to be relaxing was really a turn off. The chairs were unpadded and uncomfortable. Craig had lost weight; he no longer had much of his own padding so he wanted chairs with padding.

Finally, the nurse called him and he went through the usual weight and blood pressure routine and waited in the examination room until Dr. Birch appeared.

"Afternoon, Craig. How are you doing today?"

"I'm doing without as usual. And I have been quite dizzy lately."

"I see your blood pressure is a bit low. Let's change your blood pressure prescription to a lower strength, and that should work. How are you coming with the job for me?"

"I have altered the pills in all but two of the bottles. And those two should be complete in a day or two. It was child's play. Couldn't have been simpler. The hard part was getting to the correct pharmacy after the prescription was filled but before the customer picked them up. This required a lot more running around to the various stores than I am used to. But for one million tax-free dollars I made the adjustment and will soon be finished."

"Good news. When will you retire?"

"Actually, I am going to take a medical leave of absence instead of formally retiring. That way my health insurance and other benefits will still be fully active. Would you write me a note saying that I need to take a medical leave?"

"Sure, give me a moment and I will write it now."

Soon Dr. Birch came back with a computer form letter he signed and gave it to Craig.

"Give this to your personnel department and tell them to call me it they have any questions. You're making good progress on our project. It won't be long before the targets start dropping like flies. When you come back next week we'll see how you're doing and how the project is coming."

Chapter 13

*State Times Post News, Digital Edition:
Congressman Jindal, his wife and one member of his
family were injured in an unexplained natural gas
explosion. The assumption is that a gas company
worker caused a leak in the basement and when
enough gas was present the basement of house
exploded, practically destroying the house.
Congressman Jindal is expected to make a full
recovery. Unfortunately, his wife died.*

*However, the incident is under investigation. So
far there is no record of any reported gas leak or any
GDC Gas company employee working at the
congressman's house. Connections between the
attack and a possible terrorist incident have not been
ruled out.*

Karen was a perfectionist and could not help
cleaning her store everyday. Perfectionism is both a
gift and a curse. People who are perfectionistic
make great employees since they work hard and do
things right. But they tend to have a right/wrong,
black/white view of the world with very little gray.
Consequently, perfectionists are very difficult to
work for since you can never do a good enough job.

Karen had two clerks and a gunsmith who
seemed to be able to work for her. She decided to
continue paying them, and they still came to work
every day, getting their new knife inventory ready.

She laid off the gun range officer and the counterman who was still in training.

The shooting range hadn't been used for some time, but Karen still went through the two sound isolating doors to check it out. In the past there were always empty shell casings to clean up. Shooters were supposed to clean up after themselves and deposit the shells in the brass or aluminum bins, but there were always a bunch still on the ground for Karen to clean up. But this week there was nothing to clean.

Karen moved on to the large meeting room, and it too was already perfectly clean. Suddenly there was a loud knock on the locked glass door and Karen walked to the door. Three plain clothes agents held out their badge cases. This was the meeting that Karen dreaded. She had heard rumors from another gun-store owner that some of these agents were downright nasty and deliberately broke thing in their hunt for guns and ammo. But Karen had no choice and opened the door. Karen, trying to be friendly and soften up the enemy, gave a pleasant smile to the first agent. The agent smiled back, but there was no joy or happiness in it.

Then the lead agent, in a low but distinct voice, asked, "Karen Mehurin?"

She nodded her head, and he handed her a search warrant that named her store to be search for guns and ammunition.

Without another word they proceeded to move through the store. They didn't seem to be purposely damaging anything, but then there was the sound of breaking glass.

"I have to ask you to be more careful," said Karen.

He ran his fingers through his hair, scattering dandruff on his shoulders, and in a harsh voice said, "You are a gun-store owner so that is probable cause to suspect you of hiding guns or ammunition, and that would make you a felon. Do not interfere with our search." Karen was silent.

Before the gun confiscation law had taken effect, almost every gun store employee had a gun or two on their body. But now that the law was effective, the employees were basically defenseless and the agents knew this.

The lead agent stared at Karen. His fake smile and unblinking cold black eyes made her think of a stalking snake. He said, "We have to search you too for illegal guns. He knew she would not be armed and in the course of the search he became overly zealous. He put a hand on her breast in a bogus move to search her. But in reality it seemed to be an attempt to grope her.

Karen instinctively went to pull her pistol, but felt stupid when she realized that it wasn't there. Instead she glared at the agent but kept her voice was calm and level, "Stop. You're not going to paw me."

The agent angrily said, "Shut up. You know we have to frisk you for weapons."

"Don't touch me. You were not frisking. You were groping me, and I'm not going to take it."

Karen moved back quickly, inadvertently knocking a water glass off the display counter. It hit the ground and broke into several pieces. Angrily, she stared straight at the agent. In her loudest enraged voice, she shouted, "Hey! Stop now!"

Pointing to an overhead camera, she said, "The camera surveillance is going straight to the internet and being stored in the cloud. So far you're just barely OK but one more step and the government as well as my friends will come looking for you. Back off now!" And he did. But a slight tightening at the corners of his mouth formed a strained nervous smile as he lit a cigarette. He seemed to be oblivious to the no-smoking sign.

A short time later, Hunter knocked on the door and one of the BATF agents let him in. When Karen saw who it was her face suddenly brightened.

Hunter perceived that something was very wrong. He saw the broken water glass and stooped down to pick up a large piece. He held the glass in his hand and looked at the three agents.

They seemed vaguely ex-military. One of the agents appeared similar to an old Marine he knew who drank to much and went to seed. He was still big and intimidating, but not to Hunter. Then Hunter looked at the piece of water glass in his hand and in a very deep, loud, self-assured and commanding voice asked, "Is everything alright here?"

From the corners of his eyes, Hunter closely observed the three men. Then he focused on the familiar man who appeared both surprised and shocked at the same time.

Hunter shook his head and said, "You are someone I saw before. Weren't you a gunny on guard duty or possibly base security at the Quantico Marine Corps Base over in Virginia some years back?"

"Yes sir, I remember you too, Major. I'm with the BATF now, and we are doing a routine search."

"Good to see you again, son. But what in the world is BATF?"

"Bureau of Alcohol, Tobacco, Firearms and Explosives, sir. It used to be the ATF until the Homeland Security Act came along. That law moved ATF from the Department of the Treasury to the Department of Justice. Then the agency's name was changed to Bureau of Alcohol, Tobacco, Firearms, and Explosives."

"Okay. Carry on, Gunny. I'm going to get a mug of their great coffee. Do you want some?"

The way that Hunter was very powerful and yet at the same time serene and friendly unnerved the gunny. "Sir, thank you, sir, but no sir. We're done here. We were just going. Good to see you again, sir. Semper Fi."

Still holding the piece of glass in his hand, Hunter smiled and said, "Ooh rah."

As they left, the agents profusely apologized to Karen for any inadvertent damage. They put all the gun store's Form 4473 firearms transaction records in four big rolling suitcases and left a few minutes later. These were the customer signed forms that showed who had bought each gun. Previously this information was required to be kept at the gun stores for a minimum of twenty years. Now it would be computerized and used to determine who possibly didn't turn in their guns to the government. The government would soon have a list of every American who had purchased a gun during the last twenty years. And it would have the make, model and serial number of that gun.

With Hunter there, Karen now felt safe, so she gave the departing BATF agents a toodle-oo wave and then turned towards Hunter. "Did you know those jarheads?"

Hunter put the water glass fragment on the glass counter. "Just the one I spoke with, but I don't recall his name. He was a Marine Corps gunny, but not one of my reports. I heard that he was somewhat sadistic and therefore was having some problems in his unit. But I never heard the specifics. Apparently, they were bad enough to bust him down a rank and possibly to make him leave the Corps. Or he might have left during one of the personal drawdowns, or he might have been told to retire."

"Why did you call him gunny?"

"Gunny is Marine slang for an E-7 gunnery sergeant. I don't know his exact rank, but he wasn't a top. So using gunny gave him some respect even though he might have had a lower rank. I guess using the term gunny differentiates us from the army. And we like that."

"He sure changed his attitude when you recognized him. He was getting out of hand before you got here, and I wished I had my gun like I did in the past. But it seemed like one look at you and the agents changed their attitude 180 degrees."

"Yes. For better or worse, I often have that effect on people, especially people who knew me from the Corps. And, since I am so distinctive, he probably recognized me long before I could place him."

"Hunter, you really are a character. I never met anyone with as much power and presence as you have." Karen sensed that Hunter was a very dominant and yet a gentle man. She smiled and said, "You are lucky that you were born with that ability to command."

Hunter shook his head. "Yah, sure, that's easy for you to say, but I wasn't. As a child, I was a late bloomer, small, weak and essentially a loser. I was drifting with no plan. I am sure I was well on the road to ending up very badly.

"But after Vietnam, when my dad retired from the Marines, he finally came home to be with his family. I owe him everything. He is the one who taught me to be a man.

"My father was a captain in the Corps, and he told me the Vietnam jungle war almost killed him. His unit was in a forward position surrounded by the enemy. The enemy was so close that they were unable to get the choppers to drop them food. They were so hungry they thought of eating the dead enemy bodies that piled up in front of them. He didn't come right out and say it, but I got the impression that some of the bodies were eaten. But he survived that impossible horror and came home to me.

"He taught me about fighting, winning and commanding. I wish every child had a mentor like my father, who could explain what life is all about and how to live. I wish I could write a book or make a video that would explain it. But unfortunately, I can't. And very few young men who need one have a mentor of that caliber. That is one of our modern world's major problems.

"At least your government inspection is over and now you can move ahead and change the nature of your store."

Karen smiled again and her voice was good-humored and very sensual. "I can't tell you how happy I am to see you and also that the inspection is history."

Hunter tousled his hair and said, "Good. Let's move on with our lives."

Chapter 14

State Times Post News, Digital Edition: Congressman Matt Lewis was exiting his car to enter the 1812 Restaurant when he was stuck in the neck by a dart. Lewis tried to pull it out, but it was stuck. He was rushed to the hospital for emergency treatment. At the hospital Congressman Lewis was pronounced dead of potassium cyanide poison.

Investigators found a .50 caliber dart tranquilizer dart gun a block from the crime scene. The syringe dart is propelled from the gun by means of compressed CO_2 gas instead of an explosion. A compressed air dart gun is almost silent and very stealth.

This type of poison is relatively easy to get or make from potassium ferrocyanide and potassium carbonate. Only two tenths of a gram will usually kill a human in only fifteen minutes.

So far no suspects have been apprehended, but investigators are reviewing surveillance tapes and questioning witnesses.

Hunter had originally entered Karen's store to discuss the upcoming martial art class he would teach. He started to talk about it but Karen smiled and said, "Hey Hunter, I want to talk to you about something else first. I surf the Internet everyday while drinking my morning coffee and ran across an interesting blurb. A bid was recently awarded to renovate some of the rest rooms in the United Nations building. This seemed like a potential opportunity for someone to take advantage of the situation."

Hunter paused and turned his head from side to side. He looked puzzled but read the article on the United Nations building. "I'm not sure what you mean about a potential opportunity."

"They're going to be moving a lot of plumbing equipment into the building. We could move other things into the building. What I was thinking about was a Militia of One plan that might interest you."

Hunter looked surprised. He was unaware that Karen had any actual Militia of One activity. And he knew she had no military training. "I didn't realize you were taking part in the Militia of One uprising."

"They illegally closed my gun store, took my livelihood and my future. Of course I feel like I am part of the resistance."

"What do you propose we do?"

Karen kept eye contact with Hunter and said, "Actually, it's not quite a military plan but more of a basic concept for a plan. You, of course, would design any actual action plan." This was Karen's way of controlling a strong willed man.

"OK. Then what's your basic concept?"

"One article in the Internet news caused me to research this a little closer. The United Nations signed a contracted with Wagner Brothers Commercial Plumbing to modernize the restrooms. Are you familiar with them?"

"No, but go on."

Karen continued, "The article didn't say which of the buildings at the Turtle Bay United Nations complex in New York City will be modernized. But it did say that the work would start soon. I again tried to google for more information, but couldn't determine which building. However, which building really doesn't matter to the plan.

"The United Nations is totally against guns. In front of the UN headquarters they have a big outdoor anti-gun sculpture of a Colt Python .357 caliber revolver. This is the finest production revolver type handgun ever made. The sculpture is called nicknamed the Knotted Gun because the barrel is knotted so that the gun could not possible fire. I find that sculpture personally offensive, and it is proof that they have been trying to take our guns away long before this treaty.

"It's the power grab of the United Nations that caused this gun seizure and of course their headquarters is located in New York. If we could close them down, it would be a great motivational booster for the Militia. People would join the Militia who never thought we could possibly win this war."

"You're absolutely right. But how do you suggest we shut them down"?

"Fear works best. Some kind of bomb that damages a part of the UN and warns people not to come to work because more is coming."

"I like it. I am planning a few other things with explosives, but the UN is a great target. How do you suggest I do it?"

"An explosion that starts in one of the men's restrooms would really scare the men who control the United Nations. I suggest that you place the explosives inside the urinals. Most of the toilets and urinals I've seen have unused cavity space where explosives could be hidden, even from the installers."

Looking thoughtful, Karen added, "What a blow it would be to their subconscious manhood for their urinals to explode. They will thank their lucky stars that they were not using them at the time of the explosion. Additionally, I am willing to help pay you for the necessary expenses to make this happen"

"Only a woman would think of that. But it's a good thought. Urinals have a lot of cavity space that might be utilized. But it would cost a pretty penny to do it. The equipment, the transportation and the modifications would probably cost twenty five thousand dollars. I appreciate you offering to help pay but who would pay for the rest?"

"I would pay it all."

Hunter looked puzzled. "Did you say you would pay for everything? You lost all your money when they shut your store down. I thought you were practically broke."

"Yes, I was. But I did very well on the stock money so now I have money to invest in this venture."

"Invest? Like you're planning to actually make a profit on the United Nations explosion?

"I might. You don't understand what can be done with options in the stock market. I found out a way to get information that no one else has, and that could make me quite a profit."

Hunter looked puzzled and said, "Sounds weird. But if you've got the bucks to pay, I can get all the stuff we need. C-4 has the pliable texture of clay. We would need approximately two pounds of it per urinal. It can easily be molded to fit inside the wasted space of each urinal. C-4 is very stable, but when the shock of the detonator hits one of the urinals, the resulting shock would trigger the other nine urinals. The resulting explosion of, say twenty pounds of C-4, in an enclosed area like a restroom would likely destroy a substantial part of some United Nations building. I think it could work, and it would sure send a message."

"Then it's a go? If you let me know the exact cost and I'll get it together. We'll work on the subsequent details as we go along."

Hunter didn't answer but continued to read the article on the United Nations building remodeling.

"That's interesting. I am already working on a couple things that need explosives, and I expect to have some shortly. So I could move this plan to the head of the list, and it would fit in fine. Yes, I'm interested and might do it. Tell me more."

They phoned for a pizza, and Karen and Hunter nailed down the rest of the United Nations plan.

The Gun War

Chapter 15

State Times Post News, Digital Edition: All gun manufactures were shut down after the Supreme Court gun ruling. However, newly manufactured guns still continue to show up. A number of illegal small mini manufactures have opened up shop and are making knockoffs of the most popular guns. The latest 3-D printers have obviously been used to produce some of these guns. In other cases traditional manufacturing equipment appears to have been used.

There is no regulation, and these startups resemble the early days of alcohol prohibition. It is thought that organized crime or gangs are responsible for this illegal manufacturing. Trying to find and shut them down is proving very difficult.

Hunter phoned Wagnor Brothers Plumbing and received the name and contact information of their general manager. He bought a cheap used computer and set up a fake email address. Then he sat down at his computer and composed an email:

To: Rogerh@WagnorBrothersPlumbing

Subject: Absolutely free urinals

We have a brand new model urinal for commercial men's rooms and before mass production we are asking a few contractors to install them in public places. The touch-free urinalectronic® is the world's finest state of the art urinal.

This is a first class efficient self-flushing urinal with an electronic system that can be adjusted for optimum use. It is easy to install and surpasses the 1/2 gallon per flush ASME flush requirements.

We wish to give you ten or so of these urinals absolutely free for installation in your ongoing United Nations remodeling job. There are no strings attached, and we ask only that you install them in the United Nations job you recently won. We are looking for good international exposure for this new line of superior urinals.

Additionally, we will pay you ten thousand dollars after you fill out a simple two-page questionnaire about the ease of installation and the quality of the urinals.

These urinals normally come in 120 volt dropped down to 24-volt direct current. Other normal voltages are readily available should you prefer them. Just let me know when I call. All we need from you is for you to email us a zero cost purchasing order and we will do the rest.

I will contact you soon to ask for your agreement.

Sincerely,

Jack Duban

urinalectronic® Division

Jack-urinalectronic@yahoo.com

Hunter was happy with the email so he drove across town to send it from an anonymous coffee shop Wi-Fi. Additionally, he used a program that spoofed the internet address of the coffee shop with a random address.

The next day Hunter used a burn phone to call Roger at Wagnor Brothers Plumbing to try and secured the order. "Roger, this is Jack Duban. Did you get my email about the free urinals for the United Nations building?"

"Yes Jack, and I might be interested. First, did you say they are one hundred percent free?

"Definitely. No shipping charge or anything."

"How many urinals would you send?"

"Enough to complete one restroom. Do you have one that requires somewhere between eight and twelve urinals?"

"We have one lineup with ten." Would all ten be completely free?"

"Yes. For us it would be a normal advertising expense."

"One more important thing. Will you be able to make the ten thousand dollar check out in my personal name?"

"Oh yes. No problem. After the job is installed, we only ask you to fill out a three-page questionnaire. It is easy to complete. After that we will send you the check, made out to you, as payment for your help."

"Sounds good. We will need them in two weeks. Can you get them to me by then?"

"No problem. I'll get them to you. I will have them shipped to your attention. And thank you for working with us on our latest model urinal."

"My pleasure. Have a nice day."

Hunter smiled. It had been easier than he expected to give away those urinals. Now he hoped that everything would work out so that he could destroy one of the United Nations buildings.

Chapter 16

State Times Post News, Digital Edition: Justice Pegoraro died of a heart attack two days ago. Now investigators say he was murdered. An autopsy found two small burn marks on his chest that indicated his heart was deliberately stopped by the application of a high voltage current.

Some years ago, there were cases of similar types of murders. In one case a small boom box was converted into a deadly murder weapon. Four widely sold one million volt electric shock stun guns were hooked together in parallel This gave them four times as many amps as the single stun guns. One switch and a battery powered them.

Two sharp prongs that appeared to be antennas stuck out of the box. The antennas were eight inches apart. This meant that, when pressed against the chest, the current would go through the victim's heart, resulting in death. Normal stun gun probes are much closer together so the current will not go through the heart.

No murder weapon was found, but police have already arrested one of Justice Pegoraro's bodyguards on suspicion of murder. He claims he's innocent but the government has ways to make people talk.

Hunter lived in a well kept but old rustic house way out in the sticks. It had various negatives like the inconvenience of well water and a septic tank that needed regular maintenance. But it also had its strengths such as electricity from the utility grid and good cell phone reception and television from the dish on the roof. But above all, its major assets were reasonable pricing and very good privacy.

Hunter did not even have a mailbox on a post near the entrance to his home. He preferred to go to the post office to get his mail. Without an address, his home was not easy to find. You had to know where you were going to visit Hunter.

Trees surrounded the house and a short bending road completely hid the house from the highway. The vegetation also kept the house well hidden from Hunter's neighbors. No one observed his comings and goings. And that is exactly why Hunter liked the house and bought it.

Dirty windows, books all over, half eaten microwave dinners on the table, cloths strewn around the bedroom; it was definitely a man's cave. In the living room Hunter had dozens and dozens of clocks on the walls. But they did not all present the same time. Some even told time backwards. Time is inherently rigid and inflexible, and time is one of the big mysteries of life. But at Hunters house there were many various versions of the real time.

Hunter heard a car coming down his gravel road. It was Patrick.

"Good news," said Patrick. "My friend called and said I can pick up the C-4."

"Well done. When are you going to get it?"

"I will take a vacation day and get it tomorrow. And, if we need more, he said he might get it in a week or so. I'll pay him the money you gave me and bring it straight over here."

Hunter smiled and said, "Wonderful. I called the manager of the plumbing contractor, and he confirmed that they won the bid to install the urinals. I offered him ten free urinals. His company will probably still bill the United Nations for the equipment and installation. So his company will make more profit on the job. I explained this was an improved model and we needed the public exposure that the United Nations would give us.

"The contractor said he would use our sample urinals in one of the public restrooms so that the brand gets good exposure. All we need to do now is hide the C-4 in the urinals, install the simple electronics and deliver them to the contractor."

Patrick asked, "How did you get him to use your urinals?"

"Basically, money. After installation, I said I would mail him personally ten thousand dollars in a casher's check for his work."

"How much is the whole thing going to cost you?"

"No more than twenty five thousand, but the urinals themselves will only cost twelve thousand dollars. And ten of them weigh only slightly less than one thousand pounds. Fortunately, I have a sponsor for practically all of the money. And this project could make a really huge difference in the direction of President Cramer's gun war.

"I already ordered the urinals from the manufacture and they will be ready for pick up this

Wednesday. Then it will take no more than a week to install the C-4 and electronics. I have already wired him the funds from a fake account I set up.

"Patrick, after I finish my modifications, will you be able to take a day of vacation to pick them up from my house and deliver them to the contractor?"

Patrick wasn't sure he wanted to help any more and answered, "Let me think about it for a few minutes."

They were both silent and Patrick listened to the westerly breeze blowing the tree branches and whistling through the small openings in the houses old window sashes. A few moments later he became aware of the distant sounds of emergency sirens becoming louder and closer. He bit his lower lip and looked at Hunter, who shook his head and said, "Relax. I hear that every few days but they are not coming here. They are ambulances probably going or coming from the old nursing home a mile and a half down the road." The sirens slowly died down and all was quite except for the drone of insects and the chirping of crickets.

Patrick became cheerful again and said, "Tell me a little more how this is going to work."

"Your part would be very straight forward. You will take the ten modified urinals from my garage and deliver them to the receiving department at the plumbing contractor. Then leave. It's just that simple. There is certainly no crime in delivering merchandise. So even in the very unlikely event that something goes wrong, you are in the clear.

112

"If anything goes wrong, you will have total deniability. You just drive where you are told and deliver plumbing equipment. When you drive keep the car at a safe normal speed limit. Not too fast and not to slow.

"Actually, nothing can go wrong because the urinals will be carefully resealed in the original factory cartons. They'll look exactly like they always did except there will be a little less wasted cavity space. There is nothing that would be a crime on your part. I will rent a large white utility van for a week. For extra security I will change the van number and license plate."

"All I have to do is pick them up from your house and deliver them to the contractor?"

"That's all."

"That sounds easy enough. How are you going to modify them?"

"For now that's a need to know only question. Once they are delivered I will fill you in with many more details."

"And this will really make a big difference?"

"If everything goes according to plan it will make a really huge difference."

"Then I'll do it. But I am concerned that this could be so big that the Feds will stop at nothing to find out who we are. You have to give me your word that if this goes south and we are captured, you will say that I am completely innocent."

"I will, and we have a deal."

The Gun War

Chapter 17

State Times Post News, Digital Edition: A fire broke out at the Sun Inquirer Newspaper plant, destroying most of the facility. It was reported that a number of five-gallon gasoline containers were used to start the fire in the paper warehouse section of the plant. The huge rolls of paper ignite, and the heat consumed everything around them. The Sun Inquirer is a very liberal paper and constantly denounced the Militia of One. There are no suspects at this time.

Patrick drove over to Hunter's house to deliver the C-4. But Hunter took one look at it and said, "What the hell is this? The labels say that it is PE-4. You were supposed to get C-4."

"I knew you would say that, but not to worry. My friend said he was able to trade with a British quartermaster for this. He assured me that it is almost the same and actually even a little better. My man said he researched it and found that the British military uses an explosive named PE-4. The PE stands for plastic explosive. I also looked it up and found that its explosive characteristics are nearly identical to C-4. The only difference is that it has a slightly faster velocity of detonation. For some purposes, the faster expansion is actually a better choice than the actual C-4."

"Very good, Patrick. As usual you did a very competent job. Now we are a go to move ahead on the two jobs I am planning. I will phone you when I get all the parts and assemble them."

Hunter rented a plain white non-descript cargo van. Ten urinal boxes easily fit in the large van. It did not have the problems of a larger truck such as possible weigh stations and lower speed limits. Hunter disconnected the 3-wire GPS tracking device in the van and installed it in his own personal car. This removed the remote possibility that the movements of the van could in any way be associated with the van carrying the urinals. The rental company would be tracking Hunter's personal car, and it would not go anywhere near where the urinals were picked up or delivered. At the end of the delivery phase of the project, the GPS would be reinstalled in the van.

The next day Hunter glued on a fake beard, nose and mustache, then put on sunglasses and a baseball hat. He looked like a typical driver for a plumbing contractor. He signed a fake name on the urinal bill of lading, and the pickup went without incident.

Now the hard part started. Hunter already had the countdown chip, and timer, circuits that would send the signal to the PE-4 primers. He installed them in two of the ten urinals and put only the PE-4 in the other eight. The second timers equipped urinals wasn't actually necessary. It was just a back up in case something went wrong.

The corps had taught Hunter to be a cynic because everything won't always go as planned. So for Hunter, two separate wired urinals, each with its own timer, counter and detonator, gave the assurance he needed.

When either of the two urinals exploded, the enormous shock wave would take all the other nine urinals with them. The resulting explosion would be huge. It would destroy a major portion of the building. Depending on where the urinals were installed, the explosion could possibly destroy the entire building. In effect, it would be an explosion heard around the world.

The electronics would get its power from the existing urinal power connection. When the counter got to twenty flushes it would trigger an electronic relay. The next time the timer got to 3:13 the explosion would occur.

Hunter thought it was important to have someone else rather then himself deliver the urinals to Wagnor Brothers Plumbing. Patrick would be driving the same white utility van with fake license plates.

Hunter wanted to ensure that Patrick would not take a fall for his minor involvement in the United Nations building explosion. So Patrick was not instructed to wear a disguise but to to go as a completely innocent delivery guy trying to make a living. If anything went wrong Hunter would take the fall. But Hunter wouldn't go peacefully. He knew he would always keep fighting for what mattered. And freedom matters. It always matters. Protecting American freedom was the reason he joined the Marines. And guns were the only thing that kept people free from being the slaves of kings, queens, dictators and the American political establishment.

The modifications to the urinals and the rental van delivery went as planned. Hunter knew they would because there was no explosion yet. Everything was just normal business. But when the explosion occurred, everything would be examined to the maximum of the government's ability. They would eventually be looking at the urinals, but there was nothing that would point to Hunter. Still, Hunter knew that there was always some degree of risk. But if he succeeded it would be a huge blow against President Cramer and the United Nations' tyrannical conspiracy. It would definitely be worth the small risk he had of getting caught.

Hunter wanted to give the United Nations advance warning that they would have a huge explosion at their complex. He decided to say a bomb would be dropped so they would not look for one already installed. In this case, the threat and worry of an impending disaster would be much worse than the actually disaster.

Ideally, the message would come from the mysterious John Grayson since his was the name that the international press associated with the Militia of One. However, Hunter had no idea how to contact him. He decided to ask Karen for help and drove to her store.

"I need to get a message to John Grayson, the leader of the Militia of One. Do you possibly know a way to get a message to him?"

"There is a gun store owner, or I guess now an ex gun-store owner, I used to do business with. Supposedly he has some way of getting messages to him. Give me the message and I will try to pass it on. But I don't promise it will work."

"Understood. Just do the best you can."

Hunter went home, turned on some sixties music, sat down, closed his eyes, and lay back in his favorite reclining chair. He totally relaxed and could literally feel the bunched muscles in his shoulders loosen. He always knew that death was as close as a heart beat away. But that did not interfere with his resolve for American freedom from the enslavement and control of the unelected bureaucrats at the United Nations.

The Gun War

Chapter 18

State Times Post News, Digital Edition: President Cramer stated that his newest executive order required that all resistance to the United Nations gun safety program would be met with deadly force. He emphasized that government forces would no longer take prisoners but instead execute any militia members because they are traitors to the American Government.

"The Militia of One is ill equipped, ill trained and out-manned. There is no way they can stand up to our superior forces. In the near future I expect to be handed their unconditional surrender or receive news of their eradication."

President Cramer insisted that every good American needed to get on board with the gun safety program or risk their life and limb in a futile attempt to cause the deaths of many innocent lives. He finished by saying, "We will win, and those gun violence people will lose. They are wrong wrong, wrong."

Militia Of One

By John Grayson

"It is the duty of the patriot to protect his country from his government." – Thomas Paine

This is a warning. I was told by a reliable source that a bomb would be dropped on the United Nations.

Since 1952, the headquarters complex of the United Nations has been located in the Turtle Bay neighborhood of Manhattan, overlooking the East River. This is the facility that will be bombed.

I was also told that the bomb would be dropped at exactly 3:13 but the day was scrambled in transmission. I am giving you all the information currently available so that you can evacuate the complex and save innocent lives. There will be dark times ahead.

The Militia of One does not sanction destroying news media, which are protected by the First Amendment. We believe that the recent Sun Urban Inquirer newspaper fire was not started by one of our militia members.

"When governments fear the people, there is liberty. When the people fear the government, there is tyranny. The strongest reason for the people to retain the right to keep and bear arms is, as a last resort, to protect themselves against tyranny in government." – Thomas Jefferson

John Grayson

The Gun War

Chapter 19

State Times Post News, Digital Edition: A huge explosion rocked the United Nations headquarter complex at the Turtle Bay complex in New York. The United Nations General Assembly Building sustained considerable damage and will be closed until repairs are completed. Two security guards were seriously injured in the explosion and they are both in serious but stable condition. Another security guard had only minor injuries and was released.

The explosion occurred at exactly 3:13 in the morning. At that early hour, only the guards were present. This is the exact time that John Grayson, the leader of the Militia of One warned us about. Air security as well as ground security had been beefed up but obviously to no avail. So far there have been no statements from the United Nations.

Witness said that they were afraid this was the beginning of another Twin Towers 911 disaster. They stated that a very loud explosion shook the whole area. Part of the General Assembly Building practically fell to the ground. Within minutes of the explosion fire engines, police cars and ambulances arrived in the area. The whole scene was very confusing but there was only one explosion and over an hour later nothing else happened. Two security guards were seriously injured in the explosion but they are both in stable condition. Another security guard had only minor injuries and was released.

President Cramer was visibly upset when the entire cabinet came together to discuss the United Nations bombing. They stood as the President walked into the meeting.

President Cramer's voice was deeper than normal, "That damn Militia is a terrorist organization. Since it is already embedded within the America's system it is even more evil than those Muslim terrorists.

"Their dastardly idea of blowing up the men's urinals cannot be allowed to stand unanswered. It is a strike at our very manhood. We can't ignore this. I believe that now is the time to implement martial law and get all those illegal guns while we still have the edge. Frank, tell me your FBI team has something on whoever is behind this United Nations bombing"

Frank sounded apologetic, "Usually with something this big there is a lot of chatter that the NSA can pick up. We know, of course, that it is the Militia of One. But in this case there is nothing else. It is evident that we're not dealing with ordinary Muslim terrorists."

"So far we have no clues or credible intelligence to work with. However, our labs will be able to identify the United Nations explosives. Also, we are working on how it got in the urinals. We will eventually have something."

"Work faster because we need something now. We need a strong country everyone following my directions instead of hopelessly split and deadlocked. The country needs more control from above. I am the perfect person to exert the might of America against those who would interfere with the proper and strong government that I will lead. Those little people may think they can ruin my presidency. Well, they can't. There is no room for disobedience. In the future we need to be tougher on those captured militia and physically obtain the information about their leaders using any means necessary.

"We must arrest anyone who might have the slightest connection to their militia. It is important that we get those guns away from those cowboys.

"Jerry, you're in charge of Homeland Security. Why haven't we caught all these rebels yet? It seems like you don't know what you're doing and hoping it will turn out all right." President Cramer's eyes stared at and judged him. Jerry's face flushed under the scrutiny, and he became cautious.

"President Cramer, when we catch them they have no significant information on the militia organization. So far we have not able to find out who the leaders are. I am sure we will get a break soon, but nothing has worked yet."

"I hope you are using extreme measures to get them to talk."

After a long pause Jerry answered uneasily, "Of course we are. But I actually believe they don't know anyone else except the one or two people in their small group. As Frank said, there is no chatter except for the communications from their leader, John Grayson. We have used every method in our book, but they actually don't know. But when we catch the right person, I am sure we can get enough to take the whole organization apart."

"You best make that happen soon. Congress is a target, and they are revolting and could cause problems. Since we can't count on Congress, it is imperative that I take over this country and that the United Nations Treaty is respected and enforced. Country wide martial law seems to be the best answer.

"I would like your thoughts on how to do this. I also would like your views as to the consequences and possibility effects and problems of declaring martial law."

The FBI Director was the first to answer. "President Cramer, we have previously studied the martial law scenario and have concluded that there are not enough people in our military to place the entire country under marital law. And with much of the military refusing to enforce martial law we have far less people then we need. Instead of crushing the militia we would end up looking foolish, and it would give them more power."

The General from the Joint Chiefs nodded, "President Cramer, you have replaced the top generals, and your people will follow orders. But most of our troops would not fight because of the Posse Comitatus Act. However, I do have a suggestion that I believe will work."

"Before we go to suggestions, are there any further thoughts on declaring a national martial law?" The President looked around the table and saw that the Director of Homeland Security had something to say.

"President Cramer, I agree that a declaration of country wide martial law would be disastrous. There are over one hundred million gun owners, and each has an average of over three guns. We could never get anywhere close to collecting all of them. And the use of the necessary Gestapo-like tactics would create a violent backlash that would not be tenable. I fear it would create an atmosphere that could expand their ranks and threaten your presidency. In that type of nation wide rebellion they could win and we might be the ones who wind up dead."

"Okay, now let's get to the suggestions. General, what is your suggestion?"

"There are only two locations where the majority of attacks are occurring. They are of course Washington D.C. and New York City. I suggest we limit martial law to those two cities. We will have plenty enough personnel to do a very good job there. Also, it will look like a measured response. And we still would have the ability to add additional cities to our martial law restrictions. This would be a scenario we can positively win. Also, it would greatly weaken the commitment and spirit of the Militia."

President Cramer nodded. "So we have agreed. Make your preparations for my executive order of martial law in Washington and New York starting this Sunday."

The Gun War

President Cramer smiled, stood up and briskly walked out of the meeting.

Chapter 20

State Times Post News, *Digital Edition: President Cramer announced that starting Sunday, martial law will be declared in New York and Washington D. C. Your life will be different under the new martial law. Various civil liberties will be suspended. These include such things as the right to a public trial and impartial jury and the right to be free from unreasonable searches and seizures. Random personal and house searches will be conducted. They will be looking for guns and other items.*

Later that day the White House Press Secretary said, "President Cramer has declared martial law in New York City and Washington D.C. These are the two cities where most of the attacks have occurred. He has called for volunteers from the military to protect our country. What will it be like to live under martial law? It is still not totally clear but you can bet there will be solders everywhere. And I mean everywhere.

"Extreme travel restrictions will be put in place. House-to-house searches will certainly be conducted. What will they be looking for? Of course, they will be looking for guns. But they may also look for anything that shows any type of involvement in the rebellion against the government. It is also possible that certain bank accounts will be frozen, but this is not so likely at first".

Dr. Birch was happy that his work was over and four high-ranking government people were already dead. And there would be more because nine additional poisoned prescriptions were filled. These people could be expected to soon swallow their poisoned pill and die a day or two later. Dr. Birch had promised to pay Craig after a few of the thirteen are eliminated. So it was time for the gold.

Good to his word, Dr. Birch called Craig. "Did you get yourself a savings deposit box at your bank?"

"Yes. It is one of the lower boxes as you suggested."

"Good. Come over to my office right after twelve and I will give you the briefcase that you have been waiting for."

"I will be there. How much does the briefcase weigh?"

"It felt like forty or fifty pounds but I did not put it on a scale. So the weight should not be a major problem. I will give you the name of a few honest coin dealers who would be happy to convert some of the coins to cash."

Craig got to Dr. Birch's office at exactly noon. Dr. Birch called him into his private office and opened the briefcase. Craig's eyes were big, and his jaw dropped when he saw one million dollars worth of gold eagles that were now his.

"I don't know what to say. Seeing one million dollars of coins that are mine saves my life. Thanks Doctor, you are a man of your word."

A big smile spread across Craig's face, and he became more relaxed than he had been in years. "Now I can die in peace knowing that my family will be taken care of. This turns around my whole miserable life. My family will have enough money to live a good life." And Craig thought that now he had over fifty thousand dollars to spend on his celebration for a job well done and make his impending death easier.

But Craig was smart enough to do first things first. Craig didn't have much use for gold so he only put a quarter of it in his savings deposit box. He took the other gold coins to a coin shop and exchanged them for spendable money. Next he paid off his home mortgage and got a clean title to his family home. Then he bought his wife an annuity to augment the Sociality Security payments she would get after his death. Finally, he kept out fifty thousand dollars for his well-deserved celebration.

He thought about telling his wife about the financial arrangements he had made. But in the end he didn't. He thought it would be kinder to put the financial information with his will so that it would give some comfort to her after he was gone. And besides, it was time to celebrate and have some fun.

The Gun War

Chapter 21

State Times Post News, Digital Edition: In an emergency meeting, both houses of Congress voted to cease all enforcement of the United Nations Treaty and to reverse President Cramer's State of Emergency. President Cramer immediately vetoed the bill, saying that this was not the way to respond to criminals. Congress did not have the two-thirds majority of both houses to override the President's veto. So the bill failed.

Craig was a good and loving man. But he was also weak and his old addictions were strong. Unfortunately, he soon found himself entering the Rambino Casino in anticipation of more excitement.

This casino was designed to bring people in and keep them in. The walls had no clocks or windows. Everything was exciting and perfected to get you gambling and keep you gambling. Types of sounds, music and acoustic levels, lighting colors and intensities, spacing of machines, the height of the room and subliminal messages that go directly into the gambler's subconscious brain were just a few of the variables under intense scrutiny to maximize casino profits. The sounds, the lights, and staring at the spinning wheels while repeatedly pushing the button on the slot machine produced a trance very similar to hypnosis. This casino even used a mainframe computer to control the slot machines.

The Gun War

The computer knew Craig's profiles and his history at the casino. It automatically adjusted the slot machine's actions to give Craig the type of experience he liked while taking his money. The computer knew that Craig wanted "in the zone" fun and enjoyment, but in the end he also wanted to lose. Something in his subconscious told him he should lose.

Craig was down over twenty thousand dollars and getting tired. The rate at which he pushed the slot machine play button decreased. Also, the small hidden camera in the slot machine registered Craig with a depressed expression. The mainframe computer noticed this and soon a Good Luck Ambassador, in a very sexy outfit, came by with a free drink and a ticket for free food. Craig got his second wind and began pushing the slot machine play button at a faster rate. The casino's mainframe computer kept him hooked in the zone and excited. Three hours later Craig's entire fifty thousand dollars was gone.

Depressed, Craig left, and on the way home he stopped at Rosie's, his neighborhood bar. At the casino he didn't have much human interaction. Now he needed some and was happy to be drawn into conversation with real humans.

"Haven't seen you for awhile," said Ralph. "I thought you said the medicine you take didn't mix with alcohol."

"Yes, but I lost my entire fifty thousand dollar stake at Rambino's tonight, and now I need a drink and to be with people."

"That's a lot of money. I didn't know you had that to lose."

"I didn't, but I completed a job and got that and more."

Ralph looked at him with envy in his eyes and asked, "Where can I get that kind of job?

"I was the first and I expect will be the only person who ever had this job.

"Did you invent something?"

"No."

"Well, what then?"

"I really shouldn't talk about it."

"OK, relax. Have another drink and enjoy life. It doesn't last forever."

"Boy, do I know that." They had a few more rounds and Craig relaxed, got drunk and his tongue loosened.

"I thought you were a pharmacist."

"I am. Actually my job is district pharmacy manager for a large chain of stores."

"Well, that's too much money for a pharmacist or even a manager."

"Your right. I made the money on a part time job that I got because I was pharmacist."

"That sounds like drug money. You must have sold some drugs to some drug gang."

"No. I can't talk about it. I said way to much already. I'm going home now."

Craig paid his bill and left.

He had said just enough to effectively spill the beans about his involvement in something illegal. Unfortunately, Craig didn't know that Ralph's best friend was a cop, so the word spread. And Ralph was thinking that there was a possibility he could exaggerate Craig's statements and get one of the hundred thousand dollar rewards that President Cramer promised.

Chapter 22

State Times Post News, Digital Edition: Senator Gilbert and two bodyguards were instantly killed when a BattleHawk™ hit them and exploded. Law enforcement is reviewing all the videotapes in the area in hopes of determining the launching location of the device.

Back in 2015 the military began using the BattleHawk™ lethal miniature aerial munitions system. It is small, only 18 inches long, but has a camera and a 40 mm fragmenting grenade warhead. It can travel at 100 miles per hour and destroy a target over three miles away. Using the latest super quiet technology, the whirring of the small drone's propeller is very quiet. It operates on a, easy to us, Android-based fire control interface that can be controlled by front line troops.

This is a powerful killing machine. There is no way of taking cover from a BattleHawk™ since it can circle around and attack from any direction. This particular BattleHawk's™ origin is a mystery since the serial number was completely removed. The newer model aerial system products have serial numbers that are more difficult to remove. Also, the newer model has nano-scale particles of aluminum mixed in with a new type of explosive to produce even greater detonation force.

The Gun War

Detective Higgins and an FBI agent rang Craig's doorbell. He got out of bed and walked downstairs and opened the door.

The agents flashed their credentials. "Craig Miles?"

"Yes, what's the problem?"

"Oh no problem. We only want to ask you a few simple questions. Are you the district pharmacy manager in the DC area?

"I used to be but I'm on medical leave now."

"When did that start?"

"Recently. However, I am feeling very sick today and can't talk. What's this about?"

"We have a record of you coming into a lot of money recently. Where did the money come from?"

"That's none of your business."

"I'm afraid it is our business."

"Please leave now."

"Mr. Miles, we would like you to come down to the office and answer a few questions."

"No. This is not a good time. I'm sick and can't go anywhere."

"I'm afraid I will have to invoke the Patriot Act and insist that you come with us."

"What do you mean?"

"Mr. Miles, you are under arrest and required to come with us."

"You don't have any real reason to arrest me. I demand my rights."

"Under the martial law and Patriot Act we can arrest and hold you forever. You have no rights. You are the property of the government and you will do whatever we say."

"I can't go. I told you, I'm sick and need to take regular medicine."

"You're coming to the FBI office either willingly or forcibly. I will not take no for an answer. We will see that you get the medication you need. We just want to talk about some of the things you said the other night at Rosie's Bar." Craig's heart sank as the FBI agents put him in their car.

In the interrogation room the questioning started immediately. "Now where did that money come from?"

"As I told you, that's none of your business."

"It certainly is our business. So where did that money come from?"

Craig didn't answer so the agent left, closed the door, and Craig sat there. After what seemed like an eternity Craig started shouting. Soon a different agent entered the interrogation room.

"Where did the other agent go?"

"He went home. He must have forgotten you were waiting. Let's see, he wrote that you received a lot of money from the Militia of One. Tell me what the money was for."

"He said Militia of One? Why did he say that?

"So tell me what your function with the Militia of One was.

"I don't know anything about that Militia of One."

"It says right here that you did work for them. What does it have to do with being a pharmacy manager?"

Craig remained silent.

"If you're not going to tell me, then I'm leaving. I will have someone take you to the holding cell where you can spend the night."

"What do you mean, spend the night? I demand to go home now." But the agent just left.

When the lights went out in the holding cell Craig found it almost impossible to fall asleep. Finally he did, but he was quickly awakened by terrible nightmares. Eventually, morning came and he was exhausted. If he had some of Dr. Birch's poison, he would kill himself now.

The next morning Craig was taken back to the interrogation room, and happily there was a tray of coffee and sweet rolls. After he ate someone came in and took the tray, didn't say a word, and left.

A couple hours later yet another agent walked into the interrogation room. He sat down and gave Craig a look so deadly and so threatening that a cold shiver went down his body.

The agent sat silently, stared at Craig for five minutes, then said, "So, let's see. When you were at the pharmacy did you fill a prescription for Senator Urban?"

"No, I didn't fill prescriptions for anyone. I don't fill prescriptions. I was the district manager."

"Well, did your company fill the prescription?"

"They fill many thousands of prescriptions every day. I didn't know anything about the names of the customers. I was the district manager of five stores, for Christ sake. I hardly ever meet a customer."

"Why did you poison Senator Urban?"

Craig was silent.

"We know you did it. We only want to know why and who you had helping you."

"Helping me do what?"

"Kill those people."

"Kill what people?"

"Senator Urban. If you don't cooperate, you will die in prison. We understand that you are already dying. So, if you tell us everything, we'll recommend you for probation with no prison time."

Craig's eyes widened in the hope that he could avoid prison and the whole criminal thing. But he remained silent.

"You might as well make a deal now since you will eventually tell us. People always tell me exactly what I want to know."

"Why do people tell you?"

"Because I'm a good person and ask them nicely. If they don't tell me right away, I turn the camera off and send in someone not so nice. Then I return and they usually tell me everything. If they don't I send in the other guy a second time. Most people are quick learners and realize they will eventually talk and they might as well limit the pain they will create for themselves. So what will it be for you? Give us what we want and we will recommend no prison time. Or, be stubborn and you will eventually talk, but then you will suffer and rot in prison until you die."

Craig was easy. He was no James Bond or anything close to a super hero. He was a dying man, still trying to understand what life was all about, and why he was here. He was adverse to pain. His entire life he had taken the path of least resistance, and he rarely stood up for anything. He wasn't going to change now. He began talking.

Craig gave the authorities exactly what they wanted to know. In exchange for not sending in the bad cop and a dubious promise not to go to jail, he spilled the beans. And he also gave up Dr. Birch.

"I'm curious. How did you feel when you poisoned those people?"

"What do you mean?"

"What were your feelings? Were you sad or happy? Did you feel you did wrong or did you just feel normal?"

"Like I said, I'm dying. I didn't feel anything. For the last few weeks, Dr. Birch put me on some strong oxycodone pain pills. They mess with my mind. I'm not even supposed to drink alcohol, but I did anyway. I haven't had real feelings for some time. It's not my fault."

Craig signed the confession and was taken to jail. He objected to prison and asked when his deal would come through. But he was told that because their recommendation was not approved by the higher up powers, he would still have to go to prison.

Chapter 23

State Times Post News, Digital Edition: President Sam Cramer said, "The United States is proud to announce that we have arrested the Militia of One operative involved in the recent poisoning of some Congress members. With the death or capture of hundreds of their operatives around the country, the Militia of One has lost. We will continue to mop up all other people involved in the failed attempt to overthrow the American government.

A loud noise and multiple powerful flashlights uncomfortably shining in his eyes awakened Dr. Birch. His first thought was that this was similar to his son's last moments. Pointing their rifles, five men in black bulletproof armor stood over him. He had no choice but to give up as fast as he could.

Knowing when to fight and when to surrender saved Dr. Birch's life. The American courts are a lot more lenient than swat teams standing over you with guns. Of course Dr. Birch knew they were probably law enforcement, but his son would have had no idea that these armored intruders were not criminals.

He was arrested quietly. They asked him where he kept his guns. He told then he didn't own a gun and had never owned a gun, and didn't even like guns. He said that he was politically progressive and voted for President Cramer. They still tore his home apart, looking for any possible evidence. They found nothing of consequence.

Dr. Birch was a very smart man. There was never anything to find in his house. His pill modification was done at an apartment he had sublet under a fictitious name for three months. He did all the work there. When he left he disposed of everything. He even wiped down the apartment and left it extremely clean.

He was handcuffed and hauled down to the FBI office. They put him in a typical one-way glass interrogation room. He sat alone. It was their way of softening him up. Most people do not like long periods of silence, and when an interrogator finally comes into the room the urge to talk is typically overwhelming. They also don't like being alone and bored with nothing to do. The suspects are usually happy when anyone finally comes into the room.

After more than an hour, two agents came in. One of them asked, "How are you doing?"

Dr. Birch looked at him sarcastically and said, "Groovy, groovy, like an old time movie."

The agents looked at each other but didn't know what to say so they just stared at Dr. Birch for a few minutes until one said, "We know everything. But we still need you to fill us in on some small details. How many people are in your cell?"

"What do you mean? Are you asking how many nurses work in my office?"

"No. How many people are in your Militia of One cell?"

"I have no idea of what you're referring to. I don't know anything about a Militia of One cell."

"Cut the crap. Craig Miles told us everything. He said you got him the poison used to kill those senators and representatives. We know every little detail of your criminal operation."

Dr. Birch's upper lip twitched and his eyes narrowed. "It has been a long time since I cried because a patient didn't like me or told lies about me. I really tried to help Craig Miles, but he has a mental problem. I even decided to get him some psychological help. I suggested a psychological colleague who would see him. But he became angry and refused my help. He is not responsible for what he says. I am completely innocent of any of his rambles. My job is saving lives, not whatever he is accusing me of. I'm afraid someone who is delusional and is completely out of touch with reality has duped you. For Pete's sakes, he was so bad off, I sent him to a shrink."

"He said you send all your terminal patients to a shrink."

"That's completely wrong. I probably send way less than one percent. Most patients don't have as many psychological problems as Craig has. That's just another example of the difficulty he has with the truth. I don't know how he used to be, but for the six months I treated him he has been out there in la la land."

"Yes, but tell us about the poison."

"Craig is lying if he told you anything about poison relating to me. He is merely one of my

147

patients. He has incurable cancer and developed a very negative attitude. He was talking about killing himself by shooting himself or taking some poison. That must be where his poison fantasy came from. Because of his cancer drug regiment, Craig has become quite delusional.

"I know he thinks that it's all my fault that he is not cured. He refuses to take responsibility for his bad eating and life style habits. Instead, he blames me for not being able to cure him. Now he wants to use you to penalize me. I guess this ridicules charge is his form of punishment.

"This whole thing is without merit. Either charge me with something or let me go now. I demand that you let me talk to my lawyer."

One of the agents said, "You are being detained as a terrorist suspect and therefore you have no rights. We are going to take a break now. While were gone think about telling us the real truth when we get back."

Over two hours later an older looking special agent entered the interrogation room. "Finally," said Dr. Birch. "I'm hungry and thirsty. I need something to drink right now."

"Hello, Dr. Birch. How are you doing?"

"How am I doing? I'm doing without. I'm absolutely terrible. Craig Walker, some mentally challenged dying addict I was trying to help, claims I poisoned someone and now I'm in jail. And I already told you I'm hungry and thirsty. How the hell would you feel?"

"Well..."

"Well what? I have had just about enough of this. I want my attorney and I am going to tell him to sue you and this Gestapo organization for everything you're worth."

"But Doctor, you conspired to kill people because of the death of your son."

"My son? How dare you blame my son! Yes, my son is dead but there is no reason to compound that with these false accusations and my imprisonment. I demand, and am entitled to, a speedy jury trial. They will unanimously find me innocent."

"Mr. Walker said that you were the ringleader."

"He is certifiably crazy and, in his mind thinks, that I should have been able to perform a miracle and cure his fatal cancer. Well, I can't. Nobody can."

The agent looked unsympathetic, as if he were not even listening, and said, "Confess and we'll get you a great meal. We know you are guilty so you might as well save yourself some trouble and tell us the truth. If you keep lying you you might sit there forever."

"I have the right to an attorney. I want my lawyer now. I won't say another word until my lawyer gets here."

"Doctor, let me explain this to you again. You have no right to a lawyer or any other rights. You are a terrorist and an enemy of the state and will be treated like one."

"That is illegal," said Dr. Birch. "This feels like a witch-hunt. I demand my Fourth, Fifth and Sixth Amendment rights. I have the right to an attorney now."

"Sorry. You have no rights. President Cramer has declared martial law. Under martial law the Constitution does not apply to enemies of the State. You will do whatever we say. Or you will disappear from the face of the Earth forever."

Dr. Birch didn't say another word. He was tired of whatever games they were playing so he remained silent. Seven hours later he was moved to a private holding cell and given a meal.

But the story was becoming too big to let Dr. Birch go. The FBI wanted to show that they were making progress and winning this war. Guilt or innocence made no difference to them. He would remain in custody indefinitely.

Dr. Birch never expected this when he decided to go into the medical profession and save lives. All Dr. Birch had wanted in life was to be a good doctor and good father. But that was no longer possible. When his son was murdered under President Cramer's orders, he knew that he would never again return to his normal life. Fate had dealt him a tough hand. Unless the Militia won, he knew he would spend a long time in jail. He also knew this latest turn of events might kill him. But then, so would bad oysters. He was not afraid to die because he knew he had done the right thing. And if his dead son was watching from upon high he would be proud that his illegal murder was not committed without big time retribution. It may have been only an eye for an eye but it sure felt like justice.

Chapter 24

State Times Post *News, Digital Edition: Senator Eberstadt died ten days after he was injured. A hand grenade thrown on the speaker's platform caused his wounds. One Secret Service agent also died immediately from his wounds. The perpetrators are still at large.*

President Cramer gave his third State of the Union address to the American people. Since many people loved him and many people hated him, and the war against the political establishment was on everyone's mind; practically the entire country listened on some electronic devise.

President Cramer put on his always-contagious smile and greeted the assembled government leaders and the loyal American citizens listening everywhere.

"A roundup of the top Militia of One has drastically crippled their ability to function. These prisoners were squeezed for all their information on the Militia of One. I expect that other lower level personnel will be quickly rounded up. This is the beginning of the end for their illegal criminal organization. Already, a number of cases have been solved, resulting in recent arrests.

"Brigadier General Curtis Toomey, who once served in the American Army, was the number one traitor captured. Toomey's secret identity was John

Grayson, the leader of the Militia of One. He knew what America's plans were, and that was how the Militia was able to have some small amount of success. Additionally, he refused direct orders to deploy his men to fight the Militia. That alone is enough proof that he is a traitor. As a serving Army General, there was no trial. He received a quick execution by a military firing squad. This is the established method for military traitors during a time of war.

"With the execution of their leader plus the capture of a good many of their top operatives, the little Militia of One war is all but over. Thousands have already been arrested. They are amateurs and are no match for our superb well-trained fighters.

"Soon, the entire militia will cease to exist. We will continue to mop up any other minor people involved in their failed attempt to overthrow the elected American government. They can run but they can't hide from our loyal forces."

"Disarmament of our citizens is now settled law. A recent survey said that 97% of Americans approve of the law. It is now time for everyone to stop denying the reality of this law and turn in your guns.

"We are on the verge of a new era in American history. One where everyone is treated fairly and incomes will be more evenly distributed. This year will go down in history as the beginning of a greater America. With no guns, our streets will be safer, our police more efficient, and crime will go down. The stage will be set for further improvements that I am working on and will explain in the coming months.

"I want to thank all of you for sticking with our government during our recent troubles. Now we can continue to make life safer and fuller for every American citizen."

President Cramer left the stage to thunderous applause.

The Gun War

Chapter 25

State Times Post News, Digital Edition: President Sam Cramer said, "The United States is offering a reward of one hundred thousand dollars to anyone who turns in a Militia of One member that results in the conviction of that member. I am confident that in a short time, we will uncover the identities of every last one of their members.

"We opened a few military prisons similar to the old Guantanamo Prison and will use whatever means necessary to force Militia of One members to talk. There is proof that the so-called Militia of One was much more organized then they claim. We will get all the information out of their captured members even if it kills them."

Hunter listened to the State of the Union address and shook his head. This was the saddest Hunter had felt since his friend died in his arms in Iraq. Hunter was sure the Militia of One would win, but this Cramer victory speech changed everything.

Patrick phoned and said, "Did you hear the news about General Toomey?"

"Yes. I still can't believe it. I thought that John Grayson or Toomey would have been much harder to catch. But I guess the government is already so powerful that it can't be stopped. I'm in a bad place now. I thought for sure we would win. How could we have lost so quickly."

"Do you want me to come by?"

"No. I'm way too bummed out to have anyone around. We'll talk about this later."

The next day Hunter drove down to Karen's store to teach his martial arts class. He got there an hour early because he wanted to see what Karen made of the speech.

Just seeing Karen's smiling face was uplifting for Hunter. She was so positive about everything that Hunter wondered what planet she came from. How could anyone who loved freedom be happy after hearing President Cramer's speech?

Hunter shook his head and asked Karen, "How can you look so happy during freedom's darkest hour?"

"You know what they say. It's not over until it's over, or at least until the fat lady sings. And she hasn't sung yet."

"But they executed John Grayson. If it's not over it's almost over."

"It was only a political speech. By definition President Cramer's political speeches are not true. They are either downright lies or some words with a particular spin that obscures the truth."

"Yes, but they wouldn't have said they had executed John Grayson if they hadn't."

"They may want to believe they executed him but that does not mean that they really did."

"What does that mean?"

"I'm sure they executed someone, but they got the wrong person. Since they couldn't control him, they were probably going to execute Brigadier General Curtis Toomey anyway.

"Someone in the government probably just hung the John Grayson thing around his neck to lift the government's sagging spirits. It is fairly common in the military to tell leaders what they want to hear. Since no one has ever met John Grayson they figured they could get away with it. And if they don't they are no worse off. From the look on your face, they got away with it."

"How do you know they got the wrong person?"

"I know that is how President Cramer thinks. He is a power hungry pig who lies about everything. He thinks rules are just for us little people and do not apply to him. His whole life has been one lie after another. Many of his political speeches are made for their symbolic value and not their accuracy."

"But you're talking hypotheticals. You can't be sure they got the wrong person."

"I am positive that General Toomey was not the leader."

"But what if General Toomey was John Grayson? How do you know they got the wrong person?"

"I just know."

"You can't be one hundred percent positive."

"But I am absolutely positive."

"OK, but how can you know when no one else in America knows?

"It would break the Militia rules if I tell you that."

"I didn't see that rule."

Karen's face became placid as she said, "The government is fumbling along with no clue who or what the Militia of One is or how to stop them. The situation is unlike any they ever faced. All their lies and bluster claiming they are winning is the only thing they can think to do. When those lying elite political establishment types are cornered they just lie and lie and lie some more. If they get caught they just say they misspoke."

"Yes, but logically they are so big and powerful they are bound to win."

"Hunter, you're the person who once told me that having a leader and definite chain of command may seem like the best organization for a military unit. But things change.

"You are the one who said something like, 'It is counterintuitive, but for a gorilla unit, a distributed leadership actually makes the organization many times more resilient. You told me about the book *Starship Troopers*.'

"If there is no leader, the enemy cannot win by killing or capturing the leader. The battle will never be over as long as the government's rejection of freedom exists.

"It's the same with the Militia of One. They can never lose because there is no head to chop off. They can only win or settle for a partial win.

"But the American Government is totally based on the leadership hierarchy concept. Cut off a few heads, and they are severely crippled. And everyone knows the names of the American leaders. But the government can't find even one militia leader because there are none.

"Of course the government has a secession policy. But the new leaders may have different opinions or desires than the old. Often a change of leadership is all it takes to have a peaceful resolution of a longtime war."

It was the longest speech he ever heard Karen give. He knew she repeated what he had previously said, but the Marines are trained in military chain of command and the highest-ranking Marine gives the orders to those under him."

"OK, but how can you know when there is no denial from John Grayson and nothing else to believe?"

"It would break the Militia rules if I tell you that."

"I didn't see that rule in the first statement that John Grayson sent around."

"No, but it is an unwritten rule of gorilla war. You don't blabber what you know. Please just trust me on this."

Hunter saw himself being sent to one of those gulag Soviet style prison camps where you enter and never return. They probably call it Hotel California, except that song was about drugs. And real life is about power hungry politicians who will do anything to keep their power.

Hunter thought Karen was sincere but that she didn't really know. After teaching his martial art class he went home and turned on his smart TV. And that is when Hunter emerged from his depression and again became a believer in the Militia of One.

Chapter 26

State Times Post News, Digital Edition: In other news a new Militia of One paper was released, saying that John Grayson was not killed or captured and the war will continue forever until they win. The short Militia of One statement that was released had the correct signature and appeared to be authentic.
See the details of that paper duplicated below.

Militia Of One

By John Grayson

"As long as we have faith in our own cause and an unconquerable will to win, victory will not be denied us." — Winston Churchill

Of course, the evil empire wants to say it struck back. But all they can do is lie. I was surprised to read that I was captured and executed. However, as

Mark Twain once said, "The reports of my death was an exaggeration."

The lies and propaganda of President Cramer are unending. I am here to tell you that I am very much alive and still fighting for our freedom and liberty.

Sorry, Cramer, you can't just kill some general and say it is me. Proverbs 17:28 of the bible says, "Even a fool is thought wise if he keeps silent, and discerning if he holds his tongue."

As they say in poker, "If you've been playing with the big boys for twenty minutes and you don't know who the patsy is, you're the patsy." Cramer, you're the patsy. You can't just execute your man and say that you killed me. That wouldn't even work in the B movies. You must really be desperate.

Cramer, you opened your mouth once too often. Even if someday I am captured, it will make no difference. The government does not seem to believe it but this movement has no leadership. It is a grass roots organization that will never stop until America has the freedom and liberty guaranteed in our Constitution. Even if it takes a hundred years we will be victorious.

This government would be smart to fear the people fighting for their freedom. These people can beat the dishonest person fighting for more power or money every time. And in short order, they will.

America became the greatest country in the world because we are free and because we can count on the rule of law. The American Constitution is the glue that holds America together. But it is inevitable that strong presidents will increasingly attempt to control us. President Cramer is trying to destroy our freedom and our law. But his actions will destroy him.

America's corrupt political establishment has become clowns. America's last military victory was in 1945. The clowns didn't win in Korea, Vietnam, Iraq or Afghanistan. They stand zero chance of defeating the Militia of One.

The biggest challenge with the political establishment is distinguishing reality from their propaganda. In our new brainwashing disinformation age recognizing truth and reality is more difficult then ever. The truth is that the Militia of One is very much alive. We are winning and will continue to fight for our freedom.

The campaign to take our guns away is a maneuver for acquiring the power to rule America. Would be dictators usually force their citizens to drop their guns and surrender to their rule. But we are winning big and the corrupt political establishment is losing. So naturally their lies are getting bigger and more frequent. But lying about my death is one step too far, and now you force me to unleash the hounds of hell upon you personally.

The reason why President Cramer is afraid of guns is not my problem. Why he has hundreds of Secret Service agents with guns protecting him and wants to take my little self-defense pistol away doesn't matter. The only thing that does matter is that the Second Amendment is the law of the land.

The Gun War

If you don't like it, pass a constitutional amendment, or just get over it.

In modern war everything is possible, even the unthinkable. And that is exactly why we will win. Our Militia of One is unpredictable because each soldier chooses the target, methods and timing. Additionally, we have absolutely no target that the government terrorist can destroy that will give them any advantage. If someday I were killed, and I do not for a second believe this would happen, someone would step in and likely do even a better job than I did. The steady escalation of our numbers and types of our attacks during the coming months will guarantee our victory.

President Cramer, in the end you know you will lose. Cut your losses now and accept our generous terms. As the song says, you need to know when to hold 'em and know when to fold 'em. This is fold 'em time for you gun grabbers.

The Second Amendment is clear. The right of the people to keep and bear arms shall not be infringed. This means that the government can't take our guns. Obviously, President Cramer is acting illegally. We must defend our freedom and our Constitution against this illegal gun grab. This will not be the first or the last time that blood has flowed to defend American freedom. I know that we can and will win sooner rather than later. We shall never surrender our guns.

As you know, at exactly 3:13 AM all hell broke loose at the United Nations. The United Nation's unelected socialist bureaucrats will not be allowed to rule America. The next United Nations bomb will be dropped at exactly 3:13 in the afternoon sometime in the coming weeks. Save lives and evacuate every one of the United Nations buildings. The United Nations is unwelcome in our home of the brave and land of the free.

The gun war isn't just about guns. It is about the elite entrenched political establishment at war with the rights and liberties of the American people. It's about control of the American people. It's about our very freedom.

John Grayson

The Gun War

Chapter 27

State Times Post News, Digital Edition: Senator Schein and one of his bodyguards were found dead at the Senator's home. A Fairbairn-Sykes style commando combat knife was used to kill the bodyguard. He lay in a large pool of blood. First his kidney was punctured, and then his throat was slashed from ear to ear, cutting the carotid arteries and the jugular veins.

The bodyguard's pistol was taken and used to shoot Senator Schein twice in the heart as he slept in bed. Both the knife and gun were left in the house. Killing people with this type of knife is fairly well known and is taught by most major armies. There were no witnesses, and the police have no suspects at this time.

Hunter went from depression, to resignation and now a new and even stronger resolve to attack and win. He was ready to begin work on his most audacious idea ever. The odds of it working were small, but the odds of getting caught were also small. And if it did work it would be really big. It could even be a game changer. Even if it just almost worked, it would send shock waves throughout the political establishment.

Bulletproof vests are readily available to the public without any restrictions. Hunter acquired two of them and made the necessary modifications.

It wasn't easy because the finished product had to look professional, but there was no time limit, so Hunter slowly but surely moved ahead.

After eight years with the CIA, Roger Freeman joined the United States Secret Service, and was soon promoted for the most coveted of all assignments. He was in the Presidential Protective Division guarding President Cramer.

Hunter had briefly met Freeman during the Iraq War. He also heard the scuttlebutt that said he was basically a scumbag. Freeman was arrogant and thought he was far superior to any Marine. Hunter also heard that he was one of those people who had no money consciousness and was therefore always in debt and in need for more money. Hunter believed Freeman would be gullible to his plan to get a Secret Service agent to wear a new piece of body armor.

Hunter paid fifty bucks to a website and obtained Freeman's home address, email address, photograph, names of his three ex-wives and a number of other interesting facts about the man. Then he composed a letter that said that before mass production of the vest, Mansfield Protective Armor wanted to get some feedback from the field as to exactly what they thought of the vest.

The new vest would also have a number of desired improvements. Hunter would attach a small-concealed pocket holster to the bulletproof vest. It was big enough to accept most subcompact back up pistols. This concealed backup holster would be one of the benefits of the new vest.

Other benefits included it supposedly being tested and certification to type IV Armor piercing level. This was the highest level of protection and good enough to stop some armor piercing rifle rounds.

This vest weighed the same as the inferior lower rated Type III-A vests that were only effective against pistols. Hunter claimed that the vest was constructed with a composite ceramic plate nanoparticle bonded with a Kevlar backer. This newly patented technology would revolutionary the armor vest industry.

But by far the best benefit for the Secret Service agent would be that he would receive the vest free. On top of that, he would get money to fill out a short questionnaire after wearing the vest for seven weeks.

He mailed Freeman an official looking letter. Of course he used a fake name but threw in some old detail so that Freeman would think his made up name actually knew him from somewhere. All Freeman would have to do was phone Hunter's throwaway phone with an okay, and the vest would be sent to his home.

Hunter had previously met one other Secret Service agent. In the event that Freeman said no to the offer, the other agent would be Hunter's backup.

The Gun War

Chapter 28

State Times Post News, Digital Edition: Senator Craft's house exploded and burned down shortly after an inspection by the gas company. Everyone got out safely. The gas company claims it is unaware of an inspection or problem at Senator Craft's home. Police officials have a description of the inspector and are investigating the incident. It is believed that this was only a gas leak accident and not a deliberate explosion.

State Times Post News, Digital Edition: An unidentified person walked up to the United Nations Secretary General and his bodyguard with a fake glove over his hand and extra long jacket sleeves. Inside the glove was his Heckler & Koch 45 caliber compact pistol. He shot the bodyguard and then the senator multiple times. Then he quickly walked to his car and drove away. High-end surveillance camera caught everything and provided a valuable clue. The perpetrator was identified, but at this time the police still do not know his whereabouts.

Freeman quickly gave his approval to wearing the bulletproof vest and filling out the short form afterwards. As Hunter anticipated, Freeman was more interested in getting paid for filling out a short questionnaire then he was about the improvements in bulletproof vests. Now Hunter began working on his vest modifications.

Hunter heard a few alert beeps and immediately looked up at the monitor to see who was coming up his driveway. He recognized Patrick Sullivan's car and went to the front door to greet him.

"Hay Patrick, how are you doing?"

"A-OK. What are you up to?

"I'm just my most overreaching self. I want to eliminate President Cramer."

"Wow. Are you for real? How do you imagine you can do that?"

"You can do it for me."

"Come again?"

"Using your connections at the Jefferson Air Force Base Golf Course, we can eliminate Cramer for good."

"How?"

"All you will have to do is push a button. The rest will already be history. And you will make this history, although no one will ever link your name to Cramer.

"All I have to do is push a button?"

"I know it sounds strange. But yes, you just push a button."

"I just push a button and it kills the President?"

"Let me give you the details of what I am concocting." Hunter proceeded to give Patrick the specifics of his work for the last few days. "If you want you could also help me modify the vest."

"What do you need?"

"I don't want to use metal shrapnel in the vest because it would block the radio signal to the detonator. So I'm going to use lighter ceramic. I have a ceramic plate and I need the back of it ground down in a checkerboard pattern so that when the PE-4 explodes, the ceramic will come apart as shrapnel. So you use this router to grind away some of the ceramic."

"I'd be glad to do it."

"I will be working on the battery, timer, signal receiver and detonator connections. We should finish in a couple hours. Then I will install my electronics inside the PE-4 and start the one-week timer."

"I calculated that we need a least two pounds of PE-4 to assure a fifty foot kill zone around the explosion."

"Well, let's get to work."

Hunter's large garage was filled with the sounds of grinding ceramic, overridden by old time rock and roll tunes blasting from the four speakers.

Hunter already had plenty of the British PE-4 explosive. He had moved it from his safe and buried it on the far side of his property for safety. He retrieved a few pounds of it. PE-4 looks somewhat similar to the Kevlar commonly used in bulletproof vests. He molded the shape of the PE-4 and assembled it within a hard plastic case that was in the shape of the bulletproof vest inserts.

Hunter fit the miniature detonator, battery, receiver and timer in with the PE-4 and sealed the plastic. To conserve battery life and for safety, it was set up so that no explosion would be possible before the one-week the timer was set for. After that it would begin to listen for a radio-controlled signal needed to initiate the explosion.

The main problem was that the battery would only last only thirty-five days. After that the battery would be too weak to receive the signal. So the whole plan rested on the hope that President Cramer visited the golf course and that Freeman got within fifty feet of him. The odds were not great, but if it worked it would be the blast heard around the world.

A cell phone receiver would have been the easiest and best to use. But the Secret Service regularly scanned for electronic emissions. A cell phone works by periodically sending a signal to nearby transmitting towers letting the towers know where the cell phone is located. The Secret Service scanners would quickly become aware of this signal and discover the modified armored vest. So a receiving radio was the only way to go. Another problem was that two hundred yards is the maximum distance for the transmitter and small receiver set to work. Anything further and the signal might be too weak for the receiver to hear.

It was tedious work, but Hunter was glad to be able to make a statement for freedom. Compared to President George Washington's troops fighting the British in one of this country's coldest winters, this was nothing.

Hunter put the timer, the battery, the receiver, the detonator and the PE-4 in the fake armor plate.

After he had assembled and hooked up everything he sealed the plastic plate that completely enclosed the PE-4.

He knew that the recipient of the bulletproof vests would be near explosive sniffing dogs. Explosives have their characteristic nitrate smells, and bomb dogs home in on these. Hunter washed the PE-4 shell five times to assure that no nitrate smells would alert dog. The Secret Service dogs are German Shepherds, and the dogs and their handlers are typically well trained at Lackland Air Force Base in San Antonio.

However, Hunter also knew that these German Sheppard K-9 dogs were very smart and they would regularly allow the agents they knew to have explosives without sounding an alarm. Even though the agents had ammunition that produced similar nitrate smells and may have recently come from the shooting range with nitrates all over their cloths, the dogs did not sound an alert.

Hunter kept the name of the vest manufacturer but altered the model number so it would appear to be a new experimental model.

When they finished Patrick asked, "How did you know the Secret Service agent would accept the armored vest?"

"I didn't. If they all say no I would have nothing. But you know the saying, nothing ventured, nothing gained."

"Even though he accepted it, do you think he will actually wear the vest or will he possibly leave it at home?"

"I don't know. There are a lot of variables. Will he actually wear the vest? Will the vest explode when we want it to? Hopefully, the answers are yes. But it is a gamble. We can only try our best and see what happens.

"My guess is that it will have about a fifty percent chance of working. When you told me that you worked at the Jefferson Air Force Base Golf Course and that President Cramer often played golf there, I started thinking. That is when I dreamed up this plan. To win you have to start with what you have and improvise everything else from there. You are what I have and your position is more that I could have ever imagined. My current attack on President Cramer could only be possible with an inside connection such as yourself. I believe that if you follow instructions, your personal risk is almost zero. But you have to follow instructions closely and if you're ever questioned just plead completely innocent of any knowledge of the incident."

"Yes, sir. Remember, I am a Marine and know how to keep my mouth shut when dealing with the enemy. I will do my part."

Patrick smiled and said, "I know you will. Ooh rah."

Chapter 29

State Times Post News, Digital Edition: President Sam Cramer said, "We already have many thousands of Militia of One prisoners at various high security prisons around America. They are subjected daily to interrogations that no human can withstand for long. Many of them are talking and spilling the beans on their entire organization. Soon we will be talking about America's total victory over the Militia of One problem. Then we can get back to our common sense gun confiscation and our enlightened ban of harmful guns."

Jefferson Air Force Base Golf Course was immaculately kept. It was a well-guarded and a safe place for President Cramer to play golf. Patrick had a good well-placed friend at the base so after leaving the Corps, Patrick had become the grounds keeper supervisor. The most important part of this job was keeping the gulf course in superb condition. Patrick was good at his job and had been the supervisor for almost two years.

Patrick started using a telescope-equipped camera to take pictures of the various areas of the base that needed grounds keeper work. People became used to seeing him with the camera and paid no attention to him.

But the real purpose of the telescope was to determine when Secret Service Agent Freeman was close to President Cramer. Patrick had a photograph of Freeman, and he studied it so he could readily identify him. Hunter had told Patrick to wait until Freeman was within fifty feet or closer to President Cramer. That was when Patrick was supposed to press his small transmitter button. Hunter said that once the transmitter was pressed the explosion would be almost instantaneous.

Except for President Cramer's party and his Secret Service agents, everyone, including Patrick, was required to be completely clear of the golf course when President Cramer was playing it. So Patrick and his people went to the clubhouse.

Patrick watched the golf game through a side clubhouse window, using his telescope-equipped camera. Periodically he snapped a picture but not of the golfers. It would be of a tree or bush or anything that was not very incriminating.

Patrick waited and waited, but Freeman was not in a good position. Finally, on the tenth hole Freeman was within fifty feet of the President. The only problem was that they were near the two hundred yard limit of the transmitter.

The agent was now even closer to President Cramer and, after a second of hesitation, Patrick pressed the transmission button. He expected a large flash near President Cramer. But nothing happened. Patrick pressed it again and again and still nothing.

Patrick was aghast and wasn't sure if he had done something wrong. Thoughts swirled around in his head. Possibly the distance was to far, or maybe the agent was not wearing the armored vest that Hunter had turned into a suicide vest. And Patrick knew he was on the clock. In a few days the battery would be dead. Or maybe it was already dead?

Patrick's body began to tremble, but he was not ready to give up. He grabbed an empty cup out of the trash and walked a couple feet out the front door. His idea was to get a little closer and not behind any window that might interfere with his signal.

He pretended he was stooping down and picking up that cup to clean the lawn. After all, a good grounds keeper manager would naturally get freaked out over a piece of garbage that shouldn't be there. But hidden in his other hand he pushed the detonator button again. A bright flash immediately let Patrick know that his suspicions were correct. The aluminum screen on the clubhouse windows had weakened his transmitter signal. Now all he had to do was think about his getaway. Less than a second later he heard the sound of a huge explosion. The shrapnel and shock wave would be traveling at close to five thousand feet per second and devastate anything within fifty feet of the exploding vest. Fortunately, Patrick was about two hundred yards from the explosion and at no risk.

Patrick immediately walked back inside and went to the rest room. Safely in a private toilet stall, he disassembled the transmitter and stomped on it with the heel of his shoe. It broke into nine pieces. Then he flushed the seven smaller pieces down the toilet. There were two pieces that were too big to flush. Patrick wrapped them in toilet paper and deposited them in different trashcans.

A number of people were running towards the scene of the explosion. Patrick left the restroom and joined them. When he got as close as the Secret Service allowed, he saw the unconscious President, two civilians and five Secret Service agents lying on the ground. Two of the down agents were definitely alive and moving, but President Cramer was perfectly still. He was surrounded by multiple bodyguards seemingly waiting for the ambulance. Two of the agents administered first aid to the President. Patrick then snapped a few pictures of the disaster knowing that he might have to turn them in but also knowing that this would hint at the conclusion that he was not in any way involved in the killing of the President. And if he didn't have to turn them in, they would probably be worth a lot of money if he eventually sold them to some publisher.

Patrick walked back to the clubhouse, and no one asked why he had a camera. He took out the memory card and put the camera in his locker. He got a cup of coffee and sat down to watch what the TV had to say.

NBLL Channel 6 News Flash: We interrupt the normal programming due to the news flash coming in from our White House correspondents. There was a large explosion very close to the President. One of his bodyguards was wearing a suicide vest.

He detonated it and the President was rushed to the hospital. His condition is still unknown.

Vice President Becknell is already on his way back to Washington. Regardless if President Cramer was killed or temporally incapacitated, the leadership of America might change from President Cramer to Vice President Becknell.

Patrick bit his lip and refrained from jumping up and down in joy. But there were other people watching so instead he put on his best somber and shocked face to blend in with the expected emotional reaction of the event. How far, he wondered, has this country come when you have to kill the President to preserve freedom? But inside he smiled, knowing that he had done exactly what needed to be done. He had pushed the button and was the hero that no one would ever know about. He would be the unknown man who changed history and saved America's freedom.

Thousands of unique individual and different uncoordinated attacks are impossible to defend against. There is no rhyme or reason behind the Militia's methods. If you defeat one the others will continue. Individuality and game changing ideas can completely overwhelm and defeat the establishment's defense plans. They always had and always would. No country could protect itself against the next game changing innovation. It had become a whole new world.

The Militia of One's continuing attacks by now had targeted almost half of the politicians who had voted to confiscate America's guns. Some survived and some died, but they knew they had to stop the attacks that were targeting them. Instead of their army fighting and dying for them, they were themselves the targets of the attacks.

President Cramer had no idea of the Pandora's Box he opened when he banned guns. Now the only way for the government to stop the carnage was to surrender in some way that they could save face.

With President Cramer wounded or dead, this would be the perfect time. They could wrap all the blame for the war around Cramer. Then they could make peace with the Militia and let everyone keep their guns. They could spin it that Cramer had lost the peace but the politicians had regained it.

Chapter 30

State Times Post News, Digital Edition: President Joe Cramer was taken to Baptist Hospital where he was pronounced dead on arrival. An investigation has already begun as to how a terrorist could pose as a Secret Service agent and get an explosive vest so close to the President, who was protected by a triple contingent of Secret Service agents.

State Times Post News, Digital Edition: The suicide bomber who blew himself up and killed President Cramer is reported to be a member of the Secret Service. We will provide more information as we receive it.

State Times Post News, Digital Edition: Three hours after the assassination of President Cramer, Vice President Jerry Becknell was sworn in as the new President of the United States of America.

President Becknell addressed the nation within hours of being sworn in to his new office. In his first speech President Jerry Becknell said the political establishment is severely demoralized and now realizes that the only way to regain peace is to go back to the way things were before guns were outlawed.

He said, "The United Nations Treaty has led to the biggest American constitutional crisis since the Civil

War in 1860, and it ends now. This nation will not enforce that United Nations Treaty. Additionally, we will leave the United Nations and require that they move their headquarters out of America. Starting next week, all United National personnel will lose all diplomatic immunity. You can bet they will leave now that they are without immunity."

He stated that he never believed that the United Nations Treaty should have effected our Constitution's Second Amendment. To emphasize his point, President Becknell again said that beginning immediately he would not now or ever enforce that anti-gun treaty.

Then President Becknell shocked the country with a virtual surrender to the Militia of One. "As my first executive order I officially pardoned all Militia of One prisoners and ordered their immediate release. I will ask the Supreme Court to again rule on the Second Amendment. But regardless of the Court's decision I will issue executive orders and stand firm, and I will not enforce the United Nations Treaty. Additionally, I apologize to every family who has lost loved one in this unnecessary war. This gun war had been a terrible overreach of power by the federal government, and I will reverse it starting now."

The President went on to declare a cease-fire and truce with the Militia of One and asked that they immediately stop all hostilities. He promised to quickly move to peacefully resolve the dispute, saying that he was sure we can peacefully resolve our differences.

The President said, "I take this stand because it is the right thing to do. Our constitutional laws clearly state that people have the right to keep and bear arms. Furthermore, the majority of our population is for that right."

President Becknell again emphasized that he, like all real Americans, believes in the ten of America's Bill of Rights. He said that under his watch, the federal government would no longer be allowed to arrest an American citizen for keeping and bearing arms. He went on to say that he would also order state prisoners associated with the Militia of One to be immediately released from prisons or internment camps.

He finished by saying, "Finally, to sum it all up, I accept the peace terms of the Militia of One. I hereby pardon all participants in the recent conflict. I believe this matter is now resolved and we can move forward to make this country again the best and greatest country on Earth."

When Karen saw the news of the political establishment's surrender, she sat up straight. Her hand came up to her mouth, and the usual sounds around her went silent. Her impossible mission had worked far better then she ever hoped. She became extremely lightheaded and began sobbing. Tears streamed down her face, and her body shook. But they were tears of joy and happiness. Under the tears, she was smiling. Karen knew she had to fight back against tyranny. But she never in her wildest dreams thought the Militia of One would be able to change the world so fast and so dramatically. It was an unreal moment in her life. It was orgasmic.

The would-be dictators were defeated, and America had a new lease on freedom. She would have her gun store and her life back. Karen looked up and said, "Thank you, God. Thank you, God."

The war was over. It had lasted a little less than a year. But it changed everything we thought about small, but very specialized imbedded groups fighting in a civil war. In this interdependent electronic age, many smaller groups fighting for the same goals were demonstrably better than one larger specialized army. It would take the regular army years to reorganize and train a force that could beat this type of unbeatable insider attack.

But the regular military always prepares for the last war. The next war will be different again. And today, the direction of that difference is unknown. All we really know is that there may never be a way to defeat dedicated forces fighting for their own freedom.

Hunter was getting material together for his next mission when he heard the news of President Becknell's unconditional surrender. He was ecstatic but he was not the outwardly emotional type. Deep down he believed emotions were below the line and logic was above the line and the preferred trait for humans. He knew that logic set humans apart and made us superior to other living things. Mammals like dogs and cats felt many emotions but did not have anywhere near the logical capability of humans. Maybe politicians get elected with emotions, but wars are won with logic, planning and willpower.

Psychologists will tell you that it is not an either or situation. It is the combination that brings out our true human nature and our capacity to change our world. But Hunter believed that it was superior logic that beat the established political order and emotions had nothing to do with it.

Even for Hunter, killing the President wasn't easy. The President was undeniably evil, but he was still the President and still a human. Nevertheless, Hunter knew that Cramer had been on the verge of being another dictator so he was at peace with his actions.

In the Marines Hunter had been trained to kill. All those years of training took much of what many civilians call humanity out of him. But he rationalized that he was doing exactly what his country trained and wanted him to do. He was protecting America's freedom, and that is what he did. He was trained to protect the freedom for all Americans. Unfortunately, to do that some people had to die. That's the way it always was.

Most people probably wouldn't understand but for Hunter, war was merely war, and that meant some people had to be killed. To make a good omelet, you have to eliminate the old rotten eggs. And the death of Cramer was exactly the rotten egg that would bring peace to America. Hunter hoped that someday he could meet this General John Grayson, thank him and find out what made him tick.

The Gun War

Militia Of One

By John Grayson

It's said that, for Americans, owning a gun is what we did from the very beginning of our history. Every American knows about the settling the frontier and the cowboys and Indians. The tradition of American guns won't die easily. Neither will the desire of Americans to be free and to be able to protect that freedom.

America gained its freedom by fighting for it with a gun. We have repeatedly defended its freedom with a gun. We will always defend our freedom and never surrender our guns.

I didn't fine-tune this war. I just set the basic outline of a way to victory. Each of our untold thousands of Militia devised their own plans. No army could possibly defeat this type of attack.

The Militia of One is not only an organization but also a cause, a movement, even an idea. If I were killed and if the Militia was losing, I have no doubt that the next generation would step forward to carry on the fight. No matter what the price, Americans will defend its freedom from the tyranny of the establishment politicians or anyone else who dares to threaten it.

We expect that gun and ammunition manufacturers and the 60,000 retail gun stores in America will be immediately allowed to resume operations. That being said, the Militia of One accepts the ceasefire with the new President. However, we will keep our powder dry.

I hereby direct all Militias to stop their attacks and, if possible, to notify the new government of any time bombs that may automatically detonate in the future.

John Grayson

Chapter 31

State Times Post News, Digital Edition: People spilled out into the streets of many cities, shouting and happily celebrating the end of the civil war. Most felt that outlawing guns was unbearable to a country in love with freedom. Even though civilians were not targeted the war was still a difficult time for all Americans.

Most of the congressional establishment was also happy with the war's end. After all, if the Secret Service could not protect the President, none of them were safe.

State Times Post News, Digital Edition: A mysterious caller alerted the FBI of a bomb that needed to be defused now that the cease fire was in place. A search at the offices of Judge Don Dollbee at the Ninth Circuit Court of Appeals uncovered a booby-trap type of explosive device. It was hidden inside of a desk and was rigged to detonate upon the opening of the bottom left drawer. The device was deactivated and safely removed. The FBI said they want to thank the person who made the phone call.

State Times Post News, Digital Edition: A mysterious caller alerted the FBI of a bomb that needed to be defused now that the cease fire was in place. A search at the offices of Judge Don Dollbee at the Ninth Circuit Court of Appeals uncovered a booby-trap type of explosive device. It was hidden inside of a desk and was rigged to detonate upon the opening of the bottom left drawer. The device was deactivated and safely removed. The FBI said they want to thank the person who made the phone call.

Hunter dropped by the gun shop, hoping Karen was there, and he was in luck. She welcomed him with a big hug. She appeared happier now than he ever saw her before.

"I'm glad you came by today. The news is so great I can hardly believe it. I thought it would take at least five years. But I guess the political establishment doesn't like being a target."

Hunter had a big grin on his face. "It's amazing how many people who hate guns are happy that the Militia was eliminating the establishment politicians."

Karen smiled and replied, "It really shows what people think of the political establishment, which is not very much. It's been a long time since Americans trusted those politicians or thought they were telling the truth."

"Karen, how do you know John Grayson and exactly who is he?"

"I never said I knew who he was. No one really knows John Grayson. He simply can't be found."

"You must know. You got the information about the United Nations General Assembly bombing to Grayson in no time flat. And you knew he wasn't dead. You must either know him or know someone else who knows him or have a email address for him."

"I'm afraid that is still top secret. Like they say in the movies, it's way above your pay grade."

"The war is over. It is no longer a secret."

"But the war will some day start again. All power hungry would be dictators want to control guns. Remember what the Communist Chinese Dictator Mao Zedong said: "The communist party must control all the guns, that way, no guns can ever be used to control the party."

"But Karen, you know I am part of the Militia of One. You trust me, don't you?"

"Hunter, I already told you it is need to know only. This cease-fire may be a fake to bring John Grayson out of hiding. Or Washington may eventually try some other way to grab our guns and the John Grayson myth is what will give them pause. They know how quickly the government was brought to its knees. The very last thing those government types want is to make themselves targets again."

"Karen, you know you can trust me. Didn't I severely damage the United Nations General Assembly Building and chase those United Nations global establishment bureaucrats out of America? That was a major key to finishing this war. You just said John Grayson is a myth. Is John Grayson real, or some kind of myth, urban legend or what?"

Karen was torn between giving Hunter the information he wanted or possibly losing him as a friend. "You're right. You did prove yourself. Will you give me your Marine Corps oath not to repeat this to anyone ever?"

"Absolutely. You have my oath. I will take that information to my grave."

"Like I said, John Grayson is a myth created for security reasons. He can never be captured and tortured because he doesn't exit."

"Well, who's really in charge of the Militia of One?"

"No one is in charge. That's its strength. The government has leaders who are vulnerable, but the Militia of One has no real leadership. John Grayson can never be captured or killed because there is no John Grayson leader. That is their primary strength. Hundreds of thousands of small units, with three people or less, and no chain of command can never be stopped.

"Their second great strength is that they are already established in responsible positions throughout America. They are Militia of One sympathizers that are already infiltrated into every level of America.

"Their third great strength is that they fought for our Constitution and for freedom. The Washington political establishment only fought to protect their jobs, money and power."

Hunter looked at her in amazement. She obviously knew a lot more than he thought she would.

"So if John Grayson doesn't exist except on paper, who wrote those papers with his signatures on them?"

"Any one of us could have written those papers. That's another great strength. Now that free individuals know the power they have to protect their freedom the whole ballgame changes. Freedom will still beat democratic dictatorship, government rules and United Nations restrictions."

"I agree. But again who is John Grayson? Who wrote those Militia of One papers and distributed them across the country?"

"That information is way above your need to know. It is even higher than top secret. I told you what you asked. There is no John Grayson and there never was."

"You're right and I thank you. But my second question is who wrote and signed those papers?"

"First I need you to swear again that if I give you the name you will absolutely forever keep it secret from everyone."

"I solemnly do swear to keep it secret."

"You'll protect the secret with your life?"

"Yes. I promise with my life."

"I did." Karen whispered.

"You did what?"

"I wrote the papers. I am the fictional John Grayson."

Hunter's head shook from side to side, and his jaw dropped in disbelief. It had been many years since he was this shocked by what someone told him.

"Did..." After a long pause he swallowed with difficulty and continued, "Did you say that you are actually John Grayson? I want to clarify what you told me. Did you actually mean to say that you and you alone came up with the Militia of One idea? Are you actually that John Grayson, the leader of the Militia of One, and you wrote all the papers and changed history?"

"You got it."

"You're kidding, right?"

"I'm not kidding," she said. "I am John Grayson."

Hunter sucked in a quick breath. "Damn, I can't believe it. It's a bit hard to accept. How do I know it's true?"

Karen seemed mildly amused. "Why is it hard to believe? Someone had to do it. Who better than a gun store owner who loves her country and wants to keep it free?"

"Well, how did you sign the Militia of One papers? It doesn't look like your writing at all."

"You know of course that I am left handed. What you don't know is that my mother wanted me to be right handed so she taught me to write with my right hand. It is actually physically easier to be right handed since you pull instead of push the pen. After I moved out, I went back to using my left hand for writing because it is who I really am.

"So I used my right hand and practiced until I could sign 'John Grayson' in somewhat the style of the person's signature I was copying. It worked out great."

Hunter watched Karen's eyes, because people generally are skilled at lying with their mouth but usually their eyes betray them. But either she was very good at lying or she was telling the truth. Hunter still didn't know.

"You fooled me."

"I fooled everyone. You are the only person who knows that the right handed man by the name of John Grayson is really a left handed woman. Hunter, I really appreciate your help in this short lopsided war. It looks like I won faster than I thought I would. It's awesome. It just goes to show you, anything is possible."

"You won? Actually, I did a whole lot more to win than you. Don't get me wrong. I appreciate your support, but who did you eliminate?"

"It may seem that way to you, but you were only one of the many fighters in my war. I planned the war and in many ways I directed it."

"I didn't see you doing that much. Patrick and I and all those thousands of other fighters were the ones who won the war. We were the ones how took the risks. For God's sake, we were the ones who killed President Cramer. You have your gun store back, but we did the fighting!"

Karen laughed. "You have that view because I couldn't tell you, or anyone, my secret identity. I won and you have proven yourself. Believe me, there was a much higher price on my head than on all the other fighters put together. They thought it was so important to kill me that they killed an out of favor general and said it was me.

"I am the commander and chief. I chose the name Militia of One. I wrote all the flyers. I started everything. And I finished it."

Hunter shook his head again in disbelief. He looked at Karen and said nothing. He didn't know whether to believe her or not. He decided that he should test her to get at the real truth.

"The government has eyes and ears everywhere. How were you able to send those emails about the Militia of One without getting caught?"

"I bought six new cheap laptops. I also bought an amplified long distance Wi-Fi antenna that allows me to access a Wi-Fi signal from a half a mile away. I would park a block or two away from a coffee shop or anywhere I could get free Wi-Fi and then turned my laptop on. I used their signal and when the transmissions were over I turned my laptop off. It was easy."

"But why didn't they locate your signal while you were transmitting and before you drove away?"

"They could locate the signal but the location they got was the coffee shop, and I always parked a good distance away where there were no cameras. Also, I never used the same coffee shop twice. By the time they could get anyone to come around and investigate, I was long gone.

"In addition to turning the laptop off, the only time my Wi-Fi was ever turned on was when I was transmitting."

"Finally, just to be sure there were no cookies or other stuff I didn't want, after sending the messages, I disposed of the laptop. I took the hard drive out of the computer and hit the drive with a sledgehammer to be sure nothing could ever be recovered. I threw the bent up, useless hard drive in a commercial trash bin. Then I took out another one of those six new laptops I had bought."

"You spent a lot of money for the urinals and everything. Where did all that money come from to pay for everything?"

"There is this strange thing on the stock exchange called options. With an option you could bet one dollar and get a payoff of possibly fifty dollars. So I used an option called a put. That means if the market goes down I make a lot of money. Well, I knew the market would go down because I was going to start the Militia of One war that would drive the market down. So I bought puts. After the war got going the market went down, I cashed out my position and used the money to pay off my mortgage and for the Militia.

"The market eventually went back up. Then, when I knew the United Nations General Assembly Building would blow up, I bought more puts. This was a huge bet that the market will go down. Right after the United Nations bomb went off, the market went down to a low, and I quickly sold those options. I made a killing.

"Then after President Cramer's lies about killing me the market went way up. I bought some more puts and the next day after my response came saying that John Grayson was not really dead, the market went down. I sold those puts for even more profits. When you create the news you can make a lot of money with options. That's why there are laws against traders with inside knowledge of some company's progress. But I use Exchange Traded Funds on the whole market. They do not track only one company's stock. It is about the direction of the whole stock market. I couldn't tell you what a particular stock would do, but I could predict which way the entire market would go. And as far as I know there is no law against that."

"What are puts?"

"Puts on the Standard & Poor's 500 stock Exchange Traded Fund are bets that the top 500 stocks in America will go down in price. They are options, which are a type of derivative. In this case it was a way of selling stocks short. But it was even better than that because the gains could be magnified many times bigger with options rather than just selling stocks short. It almost seemed illegal to bet on the market going down, but it is legal and done every minute of every trading day.

"When I first heard of selling short it didn't make sense. How could you sell something you didn't own? But I researched it and then it made perfect sense.

"I recovered my huge loss on the gun store and range. I paid for some of the costs of the war. I put some money aside to improve the gun range and stock up on merchandise. And I still have a lot of money left over. I actually ended up making an obscene amount of money on this short war."

"Damn, you really are John Grayson. How did you know that President Cramer would be stubborn and not compromise right up until the end when he was killed?"

"Cramer was beginning to act more and more like a Fascist dictator. All socialist dictators are stubborn and want to take away the guns and control everything. Mussolini, Hitler, Mao, Stalin; they all wanted power."

"But I thought Mussolini and Hitler were right wing and against socialism."

"No way. They started out as far left socialists but once in power, they transformed into brutal dictators. Italy was the first country to have a party that actually called itself fascist." Mussolini was the publisher of Avanti, the official organ of the Italian Socialist Party. He said that Karl Marx was the biggest single influence of his life. He even kept a portrait of Marx hanging on his wall. Eventually, he started the Fasci di Combattimento, commonly known as the Fascist Party.

"As for Hitler, he was the head of the National Socialist German Workers Party. The word NAZI comes from the two words 'National' and 'Sozialistische', which is the German spelling of 'socialist'. As a dictator Hitler killed over thirteen million innocent Jews and others who no longer had guns to protect themselves."

"Communism is another form of socialism, and I don't have to tell you about the forty million or more unarmed people the fascist dictators Stalin and Mao killed. Stalin famously said, 'Ideas are far more powerful than guns. We don't let our people have guns. Why should we let them have ideas?'

Freedom is what makes humans great. Kings and dictators need to reduce our freedom in order to expand their power.'

"The bottom line is my plan worked. President Cramer is dead. I have my gun store back. For the trouble, cost and risk of fighting for what's right, I was fully reimbursed by the options market. And if, many years form now, a powerful establishment politician tries to grab our guns or other freedoms, there is now a blue print for future generations to follow.

"I don't think anyone will try to take our guns away ever again. But it is the natural progression for governments to want more power. And the only way for government to increase their power is to decrease the power and rights of individual citizens. So keep your powder dry because sooner or later the Militia of One will be needed again.

"According to Sun Tzu, who wrote The Art of War, the task of a winning general is to discover the enemy's Achilles heel. In this case it is that the political establishment expects power and money. But they also expect a normal peaceful life. However, the Militia of One war destroyed that normal life. The established wants to stop any war that attacks them personally."

"So you're a general now?"

"Don't worry about it, sonny. I am the person who devised the strategy to beat their four star generals. Are we clear, Major?"

"Yes, ma'am. We're clear." His gaze met hers, which for an instant expressed mischievous humor, and then became expressionless again.

Hunter always thought he was good at sizing people up and discovering their true personality. But Karen had thrown him a real curve ball. He still had difficulties believing her, but he knew it was probably true.

Karen gave Hunter a come hither look and said, "I am going to celebrate tonight. Would you care to come over to my place tonight for a bite to eat?"

Still in a daze over what to believe, Hunter nodded his head.

"I'll write my home address and phone on the back of my business card. Bring some red wine, two bottles, shall we say seven?"

Hunter took the business card, still not knowing what to say. He left the gun store muttering to himself, "Who would have thought, who would have thought?"

The Gun War

Epilogue

State Times Post News: All those arrested for helping the Militia of One were released from confinement. As they were departing, many made statements to our reporters. Dr. Birch, the high profile physician accused of killing nine government officials, said, "First the government killed my son for no reason. Then they arrested me on false charges. President Cramer had no shame. I will not shed any tears over his death."

State Times Post News: An officially signed legal document from the United Nations was personally handed to the American Secretary of State. It said, "America has not confiscated all civilian guns as their signed treaty required. Therefore, we must label America a noncompliant nation. That means they will not be a voting member of the United Nations until they uphold their treaty obligations."

Before Karen created the Militia of One there was no reason for hope. Our country was well on its way to go down the tubes to become a socialist wasteland. Some Billionaire Socialists and activists trained by Alinsky made their down payment for the Democratic Party and now own it. Saul Alinsky, whose name has become synonymous with dishonesty and evil, wrote, "Don't sell it as socialism; sell it as progressivism, economic democracy and social justice."

The Alinsky followers were trashing the American Constitution as fast as they could. But the bottom line was that socialists and communists had always known that power came from the barrel of a gun. Obviously, before they could completely burn the Constitution all opposition guns needed to be confiscated.

Karen knew that she had to do something to save America from becoming another socialist backwater like Cuba or North Korea. But the odds were way against her. The forces of freedom were on their last breath and would soon drown. She knew that she absolutely needed to keep freedom alive. That's when she remembered Geronimo.

Karen never read the *Starship Troopers* book that Hunter had mentioned. But she did intensively study Geronimo, one of the famous Apache Indian leaders. That's where she got the idea for the Militia of One, an army without a leadership structure.

A split second after remembering Geronimo, the ideas for the Militia of One mysteriously solidified in her head. It became her prime directive, and she wasted no time putting her plan into action. There was a leadership vacuum, and Karen decided to fill it.

The Militia of One had no real leaders for the government to attack. The only exception was the leader she made up out of thin air, the fictitious John Grayson. She had no desire to be famous. She wanted her gun store and her life back. She wanted the freedom that was stolen by someone's signature on a piece of paper, and Geronimo was the answer.

Five hundred years ago, the Spanish general Cortes led a small army of five hundred soldiers that captured the capital of the Aztec Empire. Their leader Montezuma controlled over fifteen million people and lots of gold. Cortes and his small group of Spanish soldiers killed Montezuma and took the Aztec gold. The small Spanish army defeated the fifteen million Aztecs.

Similarly, Spanish general Pizarro led another small army that killed Atahuallpa, the Inca leader. The Spanish defeated the Incas and took the gold.

But when the Spanish army tried to defeat the primitive Apache Indians, they failed. Even after trying for over a hundred years, the Spanish army could not defeat the Apaches.

The reason the Spanish failed was that the political power of the Apaches was not centralized. The various Apache tribes had spiritual and military leaders. But they had no central authority or chain of command. Unlike the Aztecs and the Incas, there was no chief or real leader to kill or capital city to conquer. There was no centralized political power to defeat. There was no way the Spanish could win.

The Apache military consisted of separate bands of warriors led by whichever warrior the Apaches decided to follow at the time. These Apache leaders led by example and had little power over their followers.

The Gun War

Like the Spanish, the American army also had great difficulties trying to win their Apache war. The last large band of hostile Apaches was led by the famous Geronimo.

Geronimo was driven by revenge. He was gone at the time of an attack on his camp. When he returned he found his mother, wife, and his three children dead. In retaliation, Geronimo led a series of revenge attacks. Geronimo could not order Apaches to fight. He just began fighting and others decided to join him.

Even after Geronimo was talked into surrendering in 1886, smaller bands of Apaches continued fighting for many more years. The Apaches were gorilla fighters. They avoided pitched battles unless they were superior in numbers or had some major advantage such as the element of complete surprise.

Another famous Apache leader was Cochise, and his family had also been killed. Consequently, Cochise also carried out a relentless war against Americans.

The seemingly invincible power of the Militia of One is loosely based on the model of the Apaches, especially Geronimo and Cochise. As such, The Militia of One's war with the powerful American central government was predestined to succeed, even if it took a hundred years. Fortunately, John Grayson succeeded a lot quicker.

America's heroes were always the everyday people that you would not recognize as special, but they would not give up and were willing to fight for freedom. Even the new President Jerry Becknell, understood the previously unbelievable power of the Militia of One, and the truce held. There were a few minor problems. But legislators, who wanted to stay alive, were very motivated to resolve them quickly.

America was now in defiance of various United Nations laws and treaties. The American authorities sided with the power that had come from the barrel of a revolutionary gun. Consequently, America was forced to leave the United Nations. Subsequently, the United Nations moved its headquarters to Switzerland where it already had real estate and personnel.

The short revolutionary war was over, and a free America would go on to find success, strength, greatness and glory even above that which she has already known. To paraphrase Winston Churchill, if American freedom lasts for a thousand years, men will still say, "This was our finest hour."

About Alan Fensin

Alan Fensin earned a degree in Electronic Engineering and was a design engineer working with NASA on the Apollo moon rocket that successfully allowed Americans to walk on the moon. Next he worked with Boeing in the design of the 737 aircraft. For many years he traveled to various cities giving lectures on technical aspects of Electrical Engineering.

He is the author of numerous non-fiction books and calls writing his main hobby. *The Gun War* is his first novel.